Healing Hearts

Stealing Hearts, Book 2

K. Evan Coles

D1715235

This book is a work of fiction. Names, characters, businesses, organizations, places, events and incidents either are the product of the author's imagination or are used fictitiously. Any resemblance to actual persons, living or dead, events, or locales is entirely coincidental.

This book contains erotic material and is intended for mature readers.

For information contact:
http://www.kevancoles.com

Edited by Sally Hopkinson

Book and Cover design by K. Evan Coles

Published by Wicked Fingers Press

Some hearts are made to be mended.

Zac Alvarez never expected to start his life over at forty-five, but his recent divorce means doing just that. Luckily, his career as a nurse in Boston keeps him busy and he has friends who understand Zac's need to be as careful with his heart as he is with his diet.

Acting on a whim one fall afternoon, Zac buys lunch from a food truck and meets Aiden Marinelli, a bold young chef who is taking the city's food scene in new directions. Aiden is only thirty, a fact that doesn't sit well with Zac, but both the chef and his food prove impossible to resist.

An attachment forms between the two men and, as the winter holidays draw near, Zac begins to emerge from the protective shell he's built around himself. A chance encounter with his ex-husband shakes Zac's newfound confidence, however, and he pushes Aiden away, unaware how deeply the act will hurt them both until it is too late.

Now, Zac must decide if he is brave enough to go after what he wants and mend not only Aiden's heart but his own.

Dedication

For my son, who makes me laugh every day.

Enormous thanks to Helena Stone and Shelli Pates, who generously donated their time to help fix my words, and Sally Hopkinson, my editor ninja.

You all make my stories so much better.

Contents

Acknowledgements

"Time moves in one direction, memory in another," is a quote from William Gibson's *Distrust That Particular Flavor*.

K. Evan Coles

.

"If more of us valued food and cheer and song above hoarded gold, it would be a merrier world." — J.R.R. Tolkien

"All you need is love. But a little chocolate now and then doesn't hurt." — Charles M. Schulz

·

Chapter One

Zac Alvarez eyed the cluster of food trucks through the window of the nurses' lounge, his gaze lingering on one in particular. Painted glossy black with red, green, and white accents, it was parked not far from the hospital's main entrance, its line of customers stretching as many as ten deep.

"Endless Pastabilities," said a voice behind him.

Zac's coworker, Gianna, joined him at the window, and he met her glance with a slight frown. "Hm?"

"That's the name on the black food truck," she replied. "Endless Pastabilities."

Zac read amusement in Gianna's dark eyes. "How did you know I was looking at that particular truck?"

"It's parked the closest," Gianna said. "And you told me your distance vision is junk without your glasses, so I figured there was no way you'd be able to read its name."

"Busted." Zac laughed. Gianna was fairly new to the nursing department of Mass. Eye & Ear, but she'd been easy to get to know, and Zac liked her. "You know I try to avoid the trucks entirely."

"I know you're missing out on a lot of excellent food by doing so, yes."

"It's easier to eat well if I bring food from home. Endless

Pastabilities serves Italian food, right?"

"Yes. Have you heard of them?"

"I've seen walk-up windows with that name around the city. Are they part of the same business?"

"They are, yep," Gianna said. "There's a window near Downtown Crossing, and my husband brings home takeout sometimes when we're too beat to cook. Everything I've tried has been excellent. Can I buy you lunch?"

Zac shook his head. "I'm all set with food." He held up the lunch bag he'd packed the night before. "Care to join me?

"Yes, but I have rounds first. I also think you need more than yogurt, almonds, and a teeny tiny salad today. Something hearty like a good, home-cooked meal."

"And food from a truck qualifies as home-cooked?"

"If said food comes from an Endless Pastabilities truck, then yes." Gianna swept her long ponytail over her shoulder and grinned. "Would you mind picking up an order for me? Since you're going anyway, I mean."

Zac ran a hand over his beard with a sigh. "I didn't realize I'd be going."

"Yes, you did. You just needed a little convincing."

"I suppose it'd make a nice change from salad." Zac rolled his eyes at Gianna's smirk. It'd been awhile since he'd last eaten pasta. Or anything particularly cheesy. Especially from a truck. "And since you asked so sweetly, I'll do the treating."

Fifteen minutes later, Zac had worked his way close to the front of the food truck's line. He checked his phone as he waited, and his stomach knotted when he found a message from the one person he both yearned and dreaded to hear from—his ex-husband, Edward. Zac's mood dipped and his appetite vanished, a common occurrence when Edward entered his mind. However, he knew Gianna expected an order of her favorite pasta, so he stayed in line, gaze fixed but unseeing on his phone, until a voice rang through the air.

"Hey, Doc! What can I get you?"

2

Zac stuffed his phone in his pocket. "Sorry. You caught me napping," he said.

"I'd say I caught you texting."

A young man in a black t-shirt and matching bandana tied over his head smiled at Zac from the food truck's window while people worked in the space behind him. "Have you decided what you'd like to order?"

"Oh! Yes, I have." Zac's cheeks grew warm, and he reached for the glasses in his breast pocket. "Two orders of the pasta with cheese and pepper. I'm a nurse, by the way, not a doctor."

"Those blue scrubs get me every time. Y'know, some of my favorite people are nurses," the food truck guy said before he called out over his shoulder. "Cacio e pepe, two!" He turned back to Zac. "The pasta is spaghetti today, in case you were interested. Anything else?"

"Err, yes. A house salad."

"Only one?"

"I have one already," Zac said and motioned to his bag.

The food truck guy nodded once, then turned his attention to the order. Zac watched as he portioned field greens and whisked dressing, but really, Zac was more interested in watching the food truck guy himself. He was striking with creamy skin and smiling eyes, his bone structure and features strong and elegant. Intricate tattoos stretched from under the right sleeve of his t-shirt to a few inches below the elbow, including a thick equality symbol on his inner forearm. He glanced up at Zac, and the way the right side of his mouth curled up made Zac want to smile back. For a second, Zac forgot about the message from Edward and that his legs and feet were tired from being on shift.

"Thanks, Em," the food truck guy said as another member of the crew set two steaming take-out containers on the counter. "These look great, if I say so myself."

Producing a narrow blade grater and a small block of what Zac guessed was parmesan, he garnished the hot noodles with pale curls of cheese then finished the dish with several turns from a beat-up pepper grinder. The luscious aromas that rose in the air woke Zac's forgotten hunger, and he found himself looking forward to eating much more than usual.

"Don't wait too long to eat these," the food truck guy said. He closed the tops of the brown cardboard boxes and the inked designs moved on his arm. "The sooner you tuck in, the better."

"No worries there." Zac handed over his debit card.

"I packed extra salad dressing for you, by the way."

"You did?" Zac had to smile. "Well, thank you. Is that your way of saying your salad dressing is better than mine?"

"Nope." The corners of the food truck guy's eyes crinkled with his grin. "It's my way of saying you should *try* my dressing, though, because you won't be sorry that you did."

Zac laughed. Despite the cocky words, the food truck guy's tone was sincere. "That good, huh?"

"That good. Just like everything we make on this truck." He handed a brown paper bag and Zac's card through the window. "Buon appetito."

The food truck guy wet his lips with a quick dart of his tongue, and Zac stared for a moment before he caught himself. Cheeks hot again, he turned to go.

"You come back tomorrow and let me know what you think of the spaghetti!" the guy called after him, and damn if that didn't make Zac's steps a little lighter.

He managed to wait for Gianna before attacking his food, but only just, and Zac bit back a groan as the first taste hit his tongue. "Holy hell," he mumbled around a mouthful of spaghetti.

"I told you." Gianna exuded all kinds of smug. "It's good, isn't it?"

This time, Zac waited until after he'd swallowed before speaking. "So good. I was going to save half for dinner tonight, but that's not going to happen. The guy in the truck gave me salad dressing too, and it smells fantastic. No way I need those calories on top of the pasta but—"

"I think it's vinaigrette, Zac." Gianna shrugged. "Hardly the worst thing in the world for you. Also, no talk about calories when there's perfect pasta to eat. We can worry about it later when it's time to work out."

"I can live with that, I suppose. This is probably a good time to mention that I also found some cookies in the bag." He set a small glassine paper bag between them. "They look great too, like vanilla with roasted pine nuts."

"Mmm, yeah, I've had those," Gianna said. "They're pignoli cookies. My mother loves to make them at Christmas every year, and they're delicious."

"Well, I feel bad because I didn't order or pay for these."

"No worries. They're a bonus for ordering the house special. Cacio e pepe is the owner's favorite dish, and he thanks the customers who order it with a cookie or two." Gianna smiled. "While they last, anyway."

The thought behind the simple, charming gesture made Zac smile too. "That's quirky-nice."

Gianna beamed. "Isn't it? You can give my cookie to Mark, by the way, because I won't have room after this."

"What are we giving me?" Their colleague, Mark Mannix, slid into the chair beside Zac and his jaw dropped. "Zac, you're eating food that isn't yogurt or leaves. Are you coming down with something?"

"It's my fault," Gianna said before Zac could reply. "I forced him to eat pasta and cheese from the food truck because I'm a bad friend."

Mark merely nodded, his brown hair shining under the lounge's lights. "You really are. I've always liked that about you."

"I know. So far, Zac's not complaining either, so I think we've got another convert." Gianna tipped her head at the bag of cookies. "Anyway, I'm not going to eat mine, so please help yourself."

Mark let out an "ooh" and picked up the little bag. "You know, I'd be jealous you went to that truck if I hadn't already eaten lunch, but wait 'til you try these, Zac. They're profanity-levels of good. I usually save mine and share them with Owen after work because he can't get enough of them."

The way his bright blue eyes sparkled at the mere mention of his boyfriend made Zac smile. "Take them both home," he said. "I don't need dessert after a meal like this."

"No way, man. I'll take Gianna's—thank you very much—but you *need* to eat the other." Mark extracted one cookie from the bag and set it down by his travel mug of coffee. "You won't know what you're missing if you don't."

Zac thought not knowing was rather the point, though he didn't say so. He liked knowing less about the food around him that he chose not to eat—that's what made it easier to turn down in the first place and skip eating unnecessary calories. But something about Mark's tone piqued Zac's curiosity, and that feeling was spurred on by the mix of guilt and satisfaction he was experiencing for eating a meal so much richer than his usual fare.

Tucking the glassine pouch into his lunch bag, Zac left it there until after he'd gone home. He set it on the counter after he'd emptied the bag, then put a number of miles behind him on the treadmill in his basement, tacking on five extra to make up for the pasta. He ate the yogurt and almonds he'd ignored at lunch, but in the end, all his efforts to be disciplined seemed for naught. Because when Zac finally ate the pignoli cookie, he found it perfect. Nutty and sweet, with just the right amount of chew, and a hint of orange flavor that burst onto his taste buds and made him want another. Even before he'd finished, Zac knew a second cookie wouldn't have been enough either.

Chapter Two

Zac tried not to think about pignoli cookies when he got in line at Endless Pastabilities the very next day. He also tried not to think about the healthy meal he'd packed and decided once again to ignore. The weather was quite a bit cooler, but the lines at the various trucks were no smaller, and Zac thought he read satisfaction in the friendly gaze of the guy with the black bandana.

"Back for more, I see," he said through the window. "I take it the spaghetti met with your approval?"

Zac slid his glasses onto his face. "It was very good. Best meal I've had in a while."

His words made the food truck guy beam. "I like hearing that. What can I tempt you with today? The gnocchi with pesto are especially good, if you're in the mood for dumplings."

"Sounds wonderful." Zac asked. "You don't, err, do half-orders, do you?"

"I'm sorry, we don't." The food truck guy gave Zac a rueful smile. "I'm not sure anyone's ever asked me that before."

"I'm not surprised. Still figured I'd give it a shot though." Zac ran a hand over his beard. "I'll take a regular order then and three pignoli cookies this time, please. I promised to grab some for my coworkers."

"Well, lucky for you, cookies are on the house for nurses

7

today."

Zac frowned. "What? You don't have to—"

"True, but I want to," the food truck guy said. "I told you yesterday that nurses are among my favorite people, right? That is especially true on Tuesdays in November when you are in my window." He waggled his brows, his expression so playful that Zac couldn't help laughing, even though a part of him wanted to roll his eyes at the flirty vibe.

"Be nice," a voice in Zac's head murmured. *"It's been forever and a day since someone flirted with you, and this kid is under no obligation to do so."*

That voice zapped Zac's amusement in an instant. Mostly because the voice sounded an awful lot like his ex-husband's boyfriend, but also because Zac recognized the truth in its words. It had been ages since anyone had flirted with him. Not that the food truck guy was even doing so because why would he flirt with Zac, who was only five years shy of turning fifty and starting to get salt in his beard to show for it? Regardless, playing along and being nice was in no way the worst use of Zac's time. Just like logging extra miles on the treadmill at the end of every day was fair payment for rich food at lunch.

"Thank you," Zac said. "I appreciate the gesture," he thought to add, and gladness flashed through him when the food truck guy gave him another eye-crinkling grin.

On Wednesday, Zac bought baked eggplant parmigiana from Endless Pastabilities for Mark and himself, and while they both agreed it was some of the best they'd ever tasted, the package of cookies they found in the bag definitely stole the show. This time, a smiley face had been drawn on the glassine, accompanied by the words *"Cookies Are Life!"* and the name *"Aiden,"* which Zac could only assume belonged to the food truck guy with the black bandana.

"Well, would you look at that?" A smirk pulled at the corners of Mark's lips. "I think the guy from the food truck is sweet on you, Zac. I know for a fact he doesn't draw doodles for any of the other nurses."

"How would you know such a thing?"

"Because I flirted with that kid many a time before I met Owen," Mark said, "and not once did he write his name or anything else on *my* package of cookies."

Zac frowned. "That just sounds like a euphemism for sex," he muttered, more to make Mark laugh than anything else. "Maybe you're not the food truck guy's type."

Mark snickered. "Honey, I'm everyone's type, as long as their bell swings the right way."

Zac suspected Mark was right. He was one of the most attractive men Zac knew, both handsome and charismatic and blessed with the ability to charm the paint off a wall. Up until Mark had met his partner, Owen, he'd also been the most sexually prolific man Zac had known. And if Mark had tried and failed to turn Aiden's head … well. That probably meant Aiden was involved with someone. And that he was simply being friendly toward Zac, just as he was to the other customers who visited Endless Pastabilities every week.

Zac wiped his mouth with his napkin. *Of course,* Aiden hadn't been flirting with him. He'd known that. Zac was probably twice Aiden's age, not to mention the type of guy who asked for half-portions of perfect pasta. Zac had no business even considering the possibility of flirting with someone like Aiden. They simply weren't in the same ballpark, regardless of whether the kid had a partner or not.

The next day, Zac ate the lunch he brought from home instead of going to the food truck. He was joined by Mark and Mark's brother-in-law, Keith, who also worked in their unit, and while the three shared a perfectly pleasant meal, Zac found his yogurt, almonds, and salad deeply unsatisfying. And though he hated to admit it, he knew that had as much to do with missing Aiden's smile as it did with skipping out on Endless Pastabilities's delicious food.

OoOoO

"Hey, there." Aiden greeted Zac from the food truck window on Friday though Zac thought his smile wasn't quite as bright. "I wondered if we'd see you again."

"Ah, yeah." Zac pushed his glasses up higher on his nose. "I ate food from home yesterday. Just for a change."

Aiden nodded. "How was it?"

"Adequate, I suppose," Zac said. "Shit compared to the stuff you guys are cooking though."

Aiden's eyes widened by a fraction, and then his laughter rang out. The sound set Zac off too, and their combined amusement turned people's heads all around the Endless Pastabilities truck.

"In the words of the Borg, 'resistance is futile,'" Aiden said, his eyes sparkling with enjoyment. "Hopefully, you're at least familiar enough with *Star Trek* to know what I'm talking about."

"I am, as it happens."

"Well then, this is a lucky day for both of us. How about I hook you up with today's lasagna? It's vegetable with a butternut squash béchamel guaranteed to blow your mind." Aiden leaned forward as if to share a secret. "I tested it out on some friends last weekend, and they said it was so good they almost cried."

"I'd better try it then," Zac replied. "Make it two, please, along with a salad. I owe my coworker lunch for introducing me to your food."

"Sounds good." Aiden paused in his movements. "You okay with me throwing a couple of cookies in the bag?" He raised his eyebrows a little when Zac frowned.

"Sure. Why wouldn't I be?"

"I thought maybe I came on too strong. What with my name and the smiley face on the last package." Aiden's cheeks turned pink in a way that tugged gently at Zac's heart. "I hope I didn't offend you."

"You didn't," Zac said. "You gave my friend, Mark, something to tease me about, but you didn't do anything wrong, Aiden."

Aiden gave Zac a big smile. "Cool. I'm glad to hear it."

Zac inhaled deeply and was glad when his voice remained even. "I'm Zac, by the way."

"I know."

"You do?" Unsure what to say, Zac watched Aiden's expression soften. "But how?"

"It's on your badge." Aiden gestured at the plastic card hanging from Zac's coat pocket. "I'm glad you decided to tell me on your own though."

Zac had to smile. Even if this kid was just being nice, it was pleasant to be on the receiving end. They didn't speak again until the food order was ready, but the silence between them was comfortable among the chatter of the other customers in line and the muffled sounds of the crew inside the truck.

"Here you go." Aiden handed out Zac's order, then set his elbows on the counter. "I'm not sure if you work over weekends, but you'll have to fend for yourself, I'm afraid. We handle lots of catering gigs on the weekends, so the trucks go into the garage until Monday."

"Makes sense." And it did, though Zac felt oddly deflated. "I'm off duty tomorrow, and I'll brown bag it on Sunday. Which is probably for the best considering how many miles I've had to run to work off all these good meals." Zac delighted in Aiden's scoff. "Have a good weekend, Aiden."

"You too, Zac. Don't work too hard!"

OoOoO

The following Monday, Zac found himself in line at Endless Pastabilities once more, despite the pep talk he'd given himself about cutting down on the goddamned pasta. He bought cacio e pepe for Gianna and himself, and this time, they found two crusty rolls and a container of herbed butter nestled in beside the bag of pignoli cookies.

"Oh, my God, this butter is crazy good." Gianna literally

groaned. "I'll trade you half of what's left of my noodles if you give me your roll, Zac."

Zac snickered. "Keep your pasta and take the roll. We both know I don't need bread after all this."

Her dark eyes gleamed. "Are you sure?"

"Of course. I'm good with the cookie. Which I also don't need but like even more than the crazy good butter."

She accepted Zac's roll with a sigh. "You could have both, you nerd. You're in much better shape than you actually realize."

"Uh-huh. I'll remember to ask about rolls the next time we buy from that truck," Zac said and laughed when Gianna raised one hand and pumped her fist.

"What on earth are you doing?" Mark asked, his bemusement clear as he took the seat between them.

"Gianna's having a butter epiphany," Zac told him. "There were rolls in the Endless Pastabilities bag today," he added as Gianna pushed her cookie across the table to Mark, who rubbed his hands together.

"I swear, Mark, the butter on this bread is even better than the cookies," Gianna said around another mouthful. "Heck, the bread is great too, but I wonder if they sell the butter just on its own?"

"You could always ask," Mark replied. "Or maybe send Zac to ask since the kid with the tattoo sleeve has taken a shine to him."

The tips of Zac's ears heated as Gianna glanced his way. He hadn't told her about the drawing on the cookie package. Or that he and Aiden had exchanged names. *Or* that Mark's teasing sometimes made him want to squirm.

"I'm sure the truck will sell you some butter," he said. "And bread. And whatever else you might want, for that matter."

Gianna simply nodded. "I'm sure they would too. Off topic, what are you doing Friday night?"

"Me?" Zac glanced from Gianna to Mark and back. "Um. Nothing I'm aware of. Why?"

Gianna smiled wide. "My husband, Gerrit, and I decided to have people over for Friendsgiving dinner since most of us are working the actual holiday next week. I've already asked Mark and Owen, and I already know from checking the schedule that you're off Friday night. Will you come, too?"

Zac chewed. He would indeed be working on Thanksgiving Day. It'd been ages since he'd attended a dinner party, however. Not since before Edward had moved out and that … well, Zac knew it wasn't a good sign. His stomach tightened in a very unwelcome way. The sympathy in Mark's eyes told Zac he somehow understood, and his kind smile was just the push Zac needed.

"Sounds nice," Zac said. "I'm off at five—"

Gianna didn't miss a beat. "Perfect. Be there by seven and we'll have time to chat before eating."

The knot in Zac's middle loosened ever so slightly. "Can I bring anything?"

"We're all set with food, but I'd never say no to another bottle of wine."

"She said the same thing when I asked," Mark said to Zac, who laughed when Mark aimed a pointed look Gianna's way. "What kind of party are you throwing here, girl?"

"The kind with ten people." She gave a good-natured huff. "Chances are high we'll go through more than a few bottles without even trying, so why not stock up?"

Zac sat forward as Gianna's words registered. "Ten people?" He set his water bottle down. "Gianna, you're not trying to set me up with someone, are you?"

"No. I wouldn't do that to you." Gianna patted his hand. "Gerrit and I host these dinners once a month with my brother. If you come, we'll simply have an even number of guests. There's no subterfuge or master plan, I promise."

"What if there was?" Mark asked then. He cocked his head at Zac. "You should start looking for opportunities to meet someone new, Zac, even among friends of friends."

"I'm not going to foist myself onto people I barely know, Mark."

"Why not? Isn't the whole point to get back out there and date?"

"I didn't say I was ready or even willing to get back out there." Zac sighed. "I certainly don't want to start at Gianna's dinner party. I won't even know anyone there besides you."

Mark aimed a flat stare at Gianna. "I like how he says this like it's a bad thing."

"I didn't mean it that way," Zac hastened to say, then snorted on a laugh as Mark dragged him into a hug. "Ack, no."

"Oh, shush," Mark scolded. He made a big show of messing up Zac's hair before he turned him loose. "Owen and I won't know anyone there either, besides you and Gianna."

Gianna let out a noisy sigh. "Boys, it won't matter who either of you know on Friday night because, by the end of the evening, everyone will be friends with everyone else. You'll see.

"And *you*." She shifted her focus to Zac. "You deserve a night out of your apartment and a metric ton of good food and wine."

"Amen to that." Mark gave a sharp nod. "Let yourself live a little, Zac."

A sweet ache worked its way through Zac's core. He still wasn't sure that spending Friday night at home with his cat, a bowl of air-popped popcorn, and a movie wasn't a better idea. His friends' words made sense, however. Some socializing would be a nice change.

"All right," he said with a slow nod. "I'll be there by seven."

Chapter Three

Of course, Zac's shift went sideways on Friday. He was forced to skip lunch as well as work late, and that left him hungry as he hurried first to the wine store near his West End apartment for a bottle, and then home to shower. He spent too much time fussing over his beard and clothes too, which was ridiculous given he'd looked the same for as long as he could remember and not even a nice black cashmere pullover was going to change that. All told, it was seven-thirty by the time he made it to Gianna's Victorian row house on Beacon Hill, but he still paused before he rang the bell. He wondered again why he'd come out when staying at home would have been so easy, only to laugh as the door opened and revealed Mark, hands on his hips and a big grin on his face.

"What the hell are you doing standing out there, creeper?" Mark reached out and tugged Zac over the threshold by one hand. "I'd about given up hope, you know. I was sure you'd back out too, so thank you very fucking much for proving me wrong."

Zac made a face. "Why am I not surprised you'd bet against me?"

"Because we know each other well? Besides, how close was I to winning?"

"Pretty close."

Mark kissed Zac's cheek and almost knocked his glasses askew.

"I knew it."

Zac breathed in deep. "Jesus, it smells amazing in here," he said just before Gianna appeared in the doorway.

"Oh, good, you're here!"

Zac opened his arms for her hug. "I'm sorry I'm late. Things went haywire at the start of my shift and from bad to worse by the end. You know how that is. Mark was just telling me he didn't think I'd show."

"He's been watching the door like a fucking hawk since he and Owen got here, so I hope this means he can finally relax." Gianna poked Mark in the side with her elbow and made him grunt. "Gerrit," she called and beckoned to her husband, who Zac could just see past the doorframe. "He and Mark can introduce you to everyone," Gianna said to Zac, "and your timing couldn't be better. We'll be ready to sit down for food in about fifteen minutes."

Gerrit swatted his wife's backside gently as she darted by, and then shook Zac's hand, his smile like a mega-watt bulb. "Great to meet you, Zac. Come on in and I'll get you a drink."

A glass of Cabernet found its way into Zac's hand, and a stream of names and friendly faces followed. He exchanged handshakes with Beck and Isabella as well as Emmett and Sean, and he had a moment to think Emmett looked oddly familiar before Mark's Owen was before him, his manner as charming as Zac remembered from the few times they'd met in the past. He made small talk with everyone and sipped his wine, all the while trying not to think about the empty space beside him that Edward had once filled.

"Do Gianna and her brother need any help?" he asked Gerrit. "I'm not much use when it comes to actual cooking, but I'm stellar when it comes to washing dishes."

Gerrit shook his head. "They're all set. Probably used every plate in the house, just like they always do, but we can deal with that later. Gianna prepped a bunch of stuff last night before bed, and Aiden came over after work."

Zac blinked. "Aiden?"

"Yup. He's been cooking all afternoon, and I, for one, can't wait to eat." Gerrit's glance flicked back toward the kitchen. "And hey, it looks like we're ready to go."

Zac followed Gerrit's gaze to Gianna, who stood beside Aiden from the Endless Pastabilities truck, each holding big platters of food. They both wore broad smiles, though Gianna's wavered in the face of Zac's stare.

Gerrit clapped his hands above his head. "Time to eat, guys!"

His call brought the others to their feet, and a mix of cheers and excited chatter filled the air as a mass movement began toward a long dining table at the far end of the room.

Gerrit gestured toward the platter in his wife's hands. "I'll take that, honey. Is there a lot more in the kitchen?"

"I'll grab it, Ger, no worries," Aiden said.

For just a second, Zac considered leaving. He felt foolish all of a sudden and very much like he'd been tricked as he stood there in front of Aiden, a young man he knew but also didn't. And now that Zac understood who Aiden was, he could finally place Emmett and Sean, too, because they also worked on the food truck parked outside of Mass. Eye & Ear.

So why hadn't Gianna told Zac about any of this? It's not as if she hadn't had ample opportunity over the last two weeks. She could have said something about Aiden being her brother the very first time she'd pointed Zac in the truck's direction, and especially after she'd asked Zac to dinner. Unless she thought Zac and Aiden might ... no, that couldn't be.

We've already been over this. There is no way in hell that kid is interested in you.

"Hey, Zac," Aiden said. His eyes crinkled at the corners as he flashed a familiar smile. "Gia said you'd be joining us tonight. I'm glad you could make it!"

Without the distance of the food truck between them, Zac could see Aiden was not just striking but exceptionally attractive. His eyes were a beautiful, warm hazel, and his brown hair, uncovered by a bandana at last, lay in soft curls against his head. In place of the usual black t-shirt, he wore a navy button-down, and the color put roses in his cheeks and made his lips extra pink, two things Zac really, really didn't want to notice.

"Hi, Aiden." The way Aiden's forehead creased told Zac his tone was off, and he tried to sound gentler when he spoke again. "Gianna mentioned her brother would be co-hosting dinner tonight. She didn't tell me your name or that I already knew you from the food truck, however."

Aiden's expression fell. He turned toward Gianna, whose eyes had gone wide, and the hurt on his face made guilt rise in Zac's gut. Whatever Gianna's intentions had been in inviting Zac for dinner, she obviously hadn't shared them with her brother, and Zac felt bad for assuming the worst.

"Gia." Aiden pursed his lips when Gianna held up a hand.

"Crap. This is my fault. I didn't tell you Aiden was my brother," she said to Zac, "and obviously, I should have."

"Why didn't you?" Zac asked.

"In my defense, I don't tell anyone at work that Aiden's my brother. Mark found out when he got here too." Gianna shrugged. "It gets weird when people talk about flirting with him and his general hotness, so I just play dumb."

Now Aiden frowned. "How is this now something I've done wrong?"

Gianna frowned right back. "I never said you did. You're a bit of an idiot if you haven't noticed people flirting with you though." She turned to Zac again.

"I'm sorry this got weird, but I promise it's just a misunderstanding. We're all here for Friendsgiving, nothing more or less, Zac." She set a hand on his shoulder, her touch light. "You have a bit more of a head start with some of us than with the others, but then so does everyone else depending on whom they know."

Zac nodded. Perversely, he wasn't sure if Gianna's words made things better or worse, and that was just dumb. She'd made it clear she hadn't been trying to set Zac and Aiden up, and hadn't Zac wanted to hear as much?

Gianna took the platter from her brother, her expression searching as they eyed one another, and then headed off toward the dining area. But Aiden still didn't move, and the way he looked at Zac, forehead creased while he worried his bottom lip with his teeth said a lot about how he felt about the way his sister had mishandled things.

"Sorry," he said, voice quieter than Zac had ever heard it. "I didn't know Gianna hadn't told you my name which ... Well, that makes me sound like I think everything is about me." He blew a breath out through his nose. "Anyway. I hope you'll stay. Gianna and I made some excellent food tonight, and I think you'll enjoy it."

Zac knew in his bones Aiden was being truthful. Somehow, that shifted all the awkwardness running through him into more positive feelings. Not to mention his sudden urge to erase the discomfort so clearly written on Aiden's face.

"I don't doubt I will—everything else you've cooked for me so far has been delicious." Zac gave Aiden a smile. "I'd love to stay."

"Yeah?" Some of the tension in Aiden's posture faded. "Okay, great. I guess now would be a good time to formally introduce myself again, so—" He held his hand out to Zac. "Hi. Aiden Marinelli."

"Zac Alvarez. Which you already knew from my badge."

"That I did. It's nice to meet you again, Zac." A smile crept onto Aiden's face as they shook. "I'm just going to grab a couple more things from the kitchen, so if you want to go on and sit down—"

"Nonsense," Zac said and gestured toward the kitchen. "Let me help you."

Two hours later, Zac was sure of two things: he'd been treated to one of the better meals of his life, and he'd spend the rest of the weekend working it off. He felt (almost) nothing in the way of regret.

They'd started with meatballs in marinara and oysters baked on the half-shell, then moved on to the second course—a succulent osso bucco of beef short ribs served with mounds of creamy polenta. Zac was still trying to wrap his head around how good everything was as the third course was set out, and he enjoyed every bite of the roasted artichoke salad dressed with lemon, mint, and parmesan just as much as he had the rest of the meal. By then, an idea about who Aiden Marinelli really was had started to form in his head too.

"I've never had a non-turkey Friendsgiving dinner before," he said as Aiden took his salad course plate. "Can't say I missed the turkey either. I *might* have missed the house special pasta a little bit though."

"I actually had to talk my sister out of the cacio e pepe, if you can believe it," Aiden replied. "I thought two starches seemed a bit much, and polenta suits osso bucco better. Hearing you say that, though, gives me second thoughts."

Zac's jaw dropped slightly. "Oh, God, Aiden, no. I was just joking! Please don't think anything you and Gianna cooked tonight was less than excellent."

Aiden's pleasure in Zac's words was evident in the way his eyes gleamed. "I'm glad to hear it. If you come to dinner the next time we all get together, we'll be sure to serve your favorite."

"You mean *my* favorite." Gianna poked her brother with an elbow as she passed by. "Will you get the cheese board while I make coffee?"

Ten o'clock came and went as coffee and port were served, but still the party lingered at the table, chatting over the cheeses and fruit, as well as a pear tart Isabella had baked, and Zac studiously ignored. By then, Aiden had traded seats with Owen, and he and Zac finally had a chance to chat without having to raise their voices over the table. Zac was also surprised to notice Aiden appeared tired enough to drop.

"Are you okay?" he asked. "I hope you don't mind me saying, but you look like you could use a nap."

"I could, to tell you the truth. I was up at five this morning getting ready to cook. I'll be okay though, and I can sleep in a little tomorrow. I took the day off so I could go to a friend's party." Aiden popped a blackberry into his mouth. "So you're working on Thanksgiving Day?"

"Oh, yes. A double actually," he said and chuckled at Aiden's grimace. "Pretty standard in my world. I don't have any family in town, so it's easy for me to miss out on the big meal."

"Yeah, Gianna's on duty, too," Aiden replied. "We're doing breakfast with our parents instead of the afternoon meal so she and Gerrit can be there, and we'll help my parents set up their Christmas tree."

Zac hummed. "That's nice. At least, you'll get the rest of the day off, right?"

"Well ... not quite. Endless Pastabilities is teaming up with a couple of local charities, and we'll park the trucks in a couple of places around town and serve food to people who need it." Aiden smiled. "You look like you want to ask something but don't quite know how."

"Then I guess I should just bite the bullet and ask," Zac said. "You don't just work for Endless Pastabilities, do you?"

"I'm the owner." Aiden poured more wine into Zac's glass. "Emmett's my second in command, and we started the business right out of culinary school. I got a loan to buy our first truck, and we cooked out of my apartment so we could sell spaghetti and meatballs to the stockbrokers downtown. After the catering started taking off, we bought a second truck for the hospital campus and opened a walk-up window on Washington Street. From there, it's been growing." He gave Zac a rueful smile and set the bottle down. "After the fourth walk-up window, we relocated the downtown truck to Cambridge and opened up a real brick and mortar store in Dewey Square. We call it the Test Kitchen."

Zac blinked. His suspicion about Aiden's role on the food truck had been more than answered. "Wow. That kind of growth is impressive."

"It's tiring. I like a project though."

"That's fortunate." Zac laughed. "But you must be insanely

proud."

"Oh, I am." The confidence in Aiden's voice sent a pleasant jolt through Zac.

"Do you prefer cooking in the truck as opposed to the Test Kitchen?"

"Weirdly, yes, though I do cook at the Kitchen a couple times a week, usually in the afternoons. The Kitchen is also where we have team meetings, so I'm there every day after the trucks go back to the garage. I *like* working on the trucks though, and it's a great way for me to make sure things are still going the way I want them to in the field."

"I see."

"That just makes me sound like a control freak. Which I suppose I am." Aiden wrinkled his nose. "Endless Pastabilities has been my baby for almost five years, and its success is important to me of course. I promised myself when I graduated that I'd make something of myself by the time I turned thirty or I'd go cook for someone else. And I made it, even if by the skin of my teeth."

"Such an accomplishment for one so young." Zac's cheeks heated as Aiden's mouth turned up on one side. "I'm sorry. That must have sounded unbearably condescending."

Aiden waved Zac off. "I didn't take it as such. I *am* young, I suppose—thirty only sounds old when you're under twenty-five. And running this business is a lot—being there for my teams, making sure everyone's feeling good about the work they're doing." He swirled the wine in his glass. "The decisions Em and I make … well, they make or break us, you know?"

"I do. Your parents must be proud of you too."

Aiden dropped his gaze to his glass. "I'd like to think so. I'm actually adopted, but Gianna's parents are definitely happy with the way things are working out for me. They've always been supportive, and I'm more grateful for that than I can say."

The gravity of Aiden's words was at odds with his easy tone, and Zac suspected that the topic of family was complex for Aiden. Again, he wanted to comfort Aiden, but before Zac could truly understand where the impulse had come from, Aiden had looked up and showed Zac that big, easy grin.

"Hey, the party I mentioned I'm going to tomorrow night—you want to come along?" He held up a hand at Zac's arched eyebrow. "Unless you're working of course."

"I have the day off as it happens."

"Cool," Aiden said with a smile. "We didn't get a chance to talk very much tonight, and I'd like to do that, provided you would too? Plus, Emmett and Sean will be there, so it's not as if you'd be stuck with just me."

Zac laughed softly. The idea anyone would bemoan being "stuck" *anywhere* with Aiden struck him as hilarious. And the delight that buzzed through him at being asked at all was no doubt the reason he nodded once and decided for the second time in as many days that not staying home would be a good idea.

"Give me the address, and I'll meet you there."

Chapter Four

The buzz that had nudged Zac into agreeing to go to the party with Aiden was long gone by the time he woke the next morning, and he spent most of the day fretting about whether he should cancel.

After the dinner party, he'd googled Aiden Marinelli, and now knew that he was much more than just a business owner. Aiden's public persona was closer to celebrity chef, and he was a superstar among the young cooking prodigies in the city who were taking the Boston food scene in new directions. He'd even been named by national "30 Under 30" lists multiple times and featured in dozens of Boston's food and culture magazines.

Zac had stared at the face smiling out at him from page after online page and wondered what the hell he had in common with someone like Aiden. Someone successful and well known, two things Zac was not, or at least not in the same way Aiden was.

Except … spending time with Aiden had been easy. They'd talked until the dinner party at Gianna's had broken up, and Aiden had insisted they swap mobile numbers to make meeting tonight easier. Outside of the cocksure attitude he had when it came to his cooking, Aiden had been so personable and unassuming it was as if Zac had known him for ages rather than just two weeks. That didn't make Zac's decision about going to the party or staying home any easier. Which was why he felt almost relieved when his phone chimed and his mother's name and number slid across the screen.

"Hola, Mama." Zac gave his mother a heartfelt grin the moment Marta Alvarez appeared on the screen. He and his parents messaged often, but Zac's schedule made timing video chats tricky.

"Hola, mi hijo. Que me quentas?"

"Nothing much," Zac replied in English. "What's up with you?"

"Nothing much here either, outside of getting the house ready for Christmas decorations. Your papa is out in the shed right now, digging out the decorations," Marta said, her tone and demeanor droll. "My son's steadily decreasing Spanish keeps me awake at night however."

Zac chuckled. "I'm sorry. I've been working a lot and had dinner with friends last night, which kept me out late. I'm afraid my brain is too tired to be bilingual today."

"Psh." Marta scoffed. "You would never be too tired to translate if only you would practice. But tell me, does that good for nothing ex of yours still have all his hair?"

"I couldn't say." Zac covered a smile with one hand. His mother had been seeing a psychic for over a year now, specifically because the woman had predicted Edward was destined to suffer from male-pattern baldness. "I wish you'd stop fooling around with the fortune tellers and put your money to better use."

"Eh, seeing a psychic is fun! Plus, she gives a hell of a manicure. Even if none of the predictions come true, my nails look fantastic. Who did you have dinner with last night?" she asked then, her gaze sharp and interested.

"A friend from work and her husband hosted an early Thanksgiving dinner because most of us are working that day. We had a lot of good food and wine, and I think I made some new friends too."

"You think you made new friends? Don't you know?"

"Well, I just met them so, no, not yet." A smile crossed Zac's face as he remembered Aiden's open expression. "Things look promising though. You'd have had a good time if you'd been there too."

"Mmm, are you sure?" Marta eyed Zac, wariness in the way she narrowed her eyes. "You nurses talk about the grossest things whenever you get together."

Zac chuckled at his mom's delicate shudder. "That's truer than I'd like to admit, but this dinner wasn't only for nurses so very little patient talk. We had a number of tech nerds and a graphic designer there, as well as three different chefs."

"Three! Was this party in a restaurant?"

"No, no. My friend Gianna hosted, and one of the chefs is her brother. They cooked everything in her kitchen, which still blows me away because the food we ate was truly, truly wonderful."

"Then you be careful around them, Zac. You don't want to undo all the hard work you put into keeping yourself looking so good!"

A person who didn't know Marta well would have thought she was joking by her wink. Zac knew better though. Despite the jokey manner, his mother was being deadly serious; he'd heard her warn him off rich foods too many times in his life to think anything else. He could see it in the way she was eyeing him through the phone screen too, as if making sure Zac's weight hadn't suddenly ballooned up overnight.

Zac was used to his mother monitoring his size. She did it out of love and a desire to see Zac healthy (and looking good of course). And while Zac appreciated it, he wished the attention didn't make him feel so … empty.

"I've got healthy lunches planned out for the whole week, and you know I work out nearly every day," he promised. "Everything is under control."

"Excellent." Marta's smile was fond. "Now tell me some more about these friends you may have made."

Zac did that with genuine pleasure. He told his mother about Gianna and Gerrit and Mark and Owen, as well as the guys from the Endless Pastabilities truck and how much he'd enjoyed the evening and their company. If he left out the part where he'd met Aiden and Emmett and Sean over food he'd bought from a truck, well, that was okay—Zac's mom didn't need to know every single detail about his life. Especially when it was so much easier to talk to her about Endless Pastabilities and impress her with their successes.

The talk with his mother did Zac no good when it came to meeting Aiden that evening unfortunately, and he had to force himself to leave his apartment. And though they had a nice chat on their way from Back Bay Station into the South End, the tension running through Zac must have shown on his face because it wasn't very long before Aiden stopped walking and laid a hand on Zac's arm.

"Something wrong?"

"No, not at all."

That's a lie, and you know it.

Zac hated that voice in his head. Especially when it was right. But he and Aiden were standing outside a brownstone in the South End, about to meet Aiden's friends, and Zac supposed they were probably similarly successful and well known. Which, again, made him wonder exactly what in the world he thought he was doing.

I'm spending time with a friend, he told himself, *or at least, someone who might be a friend given a little more time.*

He summoned up a smile for Aiden. "It's been a while since I went to a house party."

Aiden glanced up at the brownstone, a faint frown marring his features. "I'm not sure 'house party' is quite right. Like I said, Jace and Paul are with the Huntington Theater. They've got a show opening in a couple weeks that'll run into late December, and they always host a get-together ahead of a new show to, um, generate good energy." He cringed at his own words, and Zac covered a laugh with his hand.

"Okay, that sounds a lot weirder out loud than I thought it would," Aiden said. "But I promise it's laid back. Just drinks and snacks and lots of nerdy talk about arts and media."

"I see. And are you a theater person?"

"Oh, I'll watch theater, sure, but I get enough of playing to a crowd with the cooking, you know?" Now Aiden glanced at the streets around them before turning his focus back to Zac. "You wanna skip it? There're plenty of places we could grab a drink around here—maybe go for a walk and see if anything feels more like your scene."

"Hey, no. I won't be party to you skipping your friends' positive energy making." Zac smiled at Aiden's snicker. "Outside of the hospital, I haven't had any kind of scene in my life for a while, and I'm open to trying something new."

Aiden's friends welcomed Zac with genuine delight, which came as no surprise. Nor did the fact that many of them were a decade or more younger than Zac and impossibly vibrant, including the hosts, Jace and Paul, who seemed to take an immediate shine to him.

"I'm so happy Aiden showed up tonight," Jace said. Everything about him was warm, from his tawny brown skin to his laughing brown eyes, and he grinned big as he handed Zac a glass of Chablis. "He's skipped our last couple of get-togethers, and I was starting to take it personally."

"You take everything personally," Paul said, his tone an equal mix of affection and exasperation. Ice to Jace's fire, he was slim and blond, with a droll manner that set Zac at ease. "Aiden's just been so busy with work we hardly see him anymore," he said to Zac. "Thanks for getting him to show his face again."

Zac shook his head. "I sincerely doubt I had anything to do with it. Aiden and I literally met two weeks ago, and our first conversation that didn't start with me ordering food happened last night. I'm not sure that's long enough to even be considered friends."

"Oh, sure it is," Jace said. "This is Aiden we're talking about, after all."

"True." Paul chuckled. "That boy makes friends every time he leaves his apartment, and I don't even think he tries."

"And yet he is still single," Jace added.

Paul rolled his eyes. "Aiden seems perfectly happy with that, my darling. Not everyone wants to couple up."

Those words bounced around Zac's head as he listened to Jace and Paul chat. Just like the Friendsgiving dinner, everyone at the party except for Zac and Aiden was part of a pair—or in at least one case, a triad. And that was sort of odd. Watching Aiden move in and out of the groups of stylishly dressed people, interested in everyone and everything being said, it seemed impossible to Zac that someone wouldn't have snapped him up by now.

So maybe Aiden didn't want to be snapped up. Maybe Paul was right, and Aiden was happy not settling down into a relationship the way everyone else in the world around Zac seemed to have done. People didn't always want to couple up.

That might be true. But you certainly do. And it's not going to happen with that kid.

Well, obviously. Zac hadn't considered the possibility. Especially now that he had a better understanding of who Aiden was and the circles of people he moved among out there in the world. Zac wasn't interested in Aiden other than as a friend.

Except ...

If Zac was being honest, his interest in Aiden went beyond friendly. He'd been drawn to Aiden from almost the moment they met. And the more they got to know each other, the more Zac liked him. A reality that did Zac no favors.

"There you are." Aiden was smiling in the doorway when Zac turned to meet his gaze. "I thought maybe you'd gotten bored and ditched me after all."

Heat crawled up the back of Zac's shirt collar. "I wouldn't do that," he said, his tone so stiff that the humor in Aiden's face faded.

Goddamn it, Zac. You really suck at this.

Jace's and Paul's concern was practically palpable as Zac excused himself, but Aiden didn't say a word. Zac found a bathroom and shut himself in. He set his hands on the counter and studied himself in the mirror, waiting for his heart to stop thumping like it was about to beat its way out of him. Under the beard, he was pale from being inside so much, and the dark eyes staring back at Zac from behind his glasses were tired despite the extra sleep he'd gotten that morning. His efforts to figure out how to say goodnight to Aiden and his hosts without making more of an ass of himself weren't going anywhere either, and he cringed when a knock sounded at the door.

Of course, Aiden stood on the other side, and though Zac's insides were curling with embarrassment, he quickly opened the door wider and stepped back so Aiden could slip in too.

"I'm sorry about that." Zac waved at the apartment beyond the bathroom's walls, his mood tanking further at the wariness he read in Aiden's features. "I didn't mean to act like such an ass."

"You didn't. You took me off guard though," Aiden said. "I only meant to tease. I didn't really think you'd leave without saying goodbye."

"As I said, I wouldn't."

"Okay. So, what was that about?"

"Why are you still single?" Zac grimaced at the surprise that streaked across Aiden's face. "Shit, I'm being rude—"

"No, it's okay. Um. Well, the answer is sort of complicated."

"You don't have to explain."

"I don't mind. I'm just never sure how people are going to react when I say that I don't date much." The corners of his mouth quirked up. "Take now, for instance, and the way you're looking at me like I just said something totally mind-boggling."

Zac nodded. He knew his eyes had gone wide at Aiden's words. "In my defense, you *did* surprise me," he said. "'I don't date much' aren't words I'd have expected you to say."

"That's very flattering." Aiden's smile got softer and more real. "It's not for lack of opportunity, which I know sounds conceited—"

"Oh, I have no trouble believing it." Zac chuckled. This kid obviously didn't check himself in the mirror very much. "So, is the problem finding the right match?"

"I've never viewed it as a problem, per se, but I suppose that's accurate."

"Okay, so no dating."

"*Some* dating, "Aiden said. "It'd be a lie to say there was no dating at all. None of the dates … spark, if you know what I mean, so I end up with a lot of friends."

"Are you demi?" Zac shrugged when Aiden blinked at him. "I know there're a lot of letters in the quilt bag for a reason."

"That's fair." Aiden laughed. "I've never identified as being demisexual, but I suppose it's possible." He shrugged too. "I don't think about it much either, probably because when I *do* connect with someone, it's good. Em's the last guy I had that with."

Now Zac was the one who blinked. "Em as in Emmett? Your business partner and second in command at Endless Pastabilities?"

"Yup. We were together a couple of years, and it was a lot of fun, but things just ran their course. I'd started the business, and Em and I were working all the time … I guess you could say we became roommates more than boyfriends." Aiden licked his lips. "We ended it with the understanding we'd stay friends. Turns out we're actually *fantastic* as friends, which is fortunate given Em's such a big part of my life."

"That's impressive." Zac shrugged at the question in Aiden's eyes. "The last man I had a relationship with is someone who works at my hospital. We can hardly stand to be in the same building, never mind a tiny space like a food truck."

Aiden winced. "Ouch. That's hard."

"Luckily, it's easy for us to avoid each other. Edward works in the administrative offices whereas I'm with the patients, so it's rare we need to interface."

"Interface—I like that." Aiden snickered. "Obviously, Em and I didn't have the luxury of lots of space, but in the end, that was okay."

"I'm glad it worked out. And you haven't had a boyfriend since then?"

"No." Aiden cast his gaze at the floor. "Just haven't found the right man, I guess."

Zac bit his lip at the color that rose in Aiden's cheeks. "I didn't mean to—" He paused when another knock sounded at the door.

"Um, guys?" Paul called, his voice slightly muffled. "Is everything okay in there? You're not, like, trying to drown each other in my toilet or getting naked, right?"

Aiden shared a smile with Zac. "No one's being drowned," he called back. "And it's none of your business how naked Zac and I are, but we'll be right out." His face grew sober again. "Are we okay?"

"We're okay. Actually, you're fine, Aiden. It's me who's the problem."

"Bit soon to be using an 'it's not you it's me' kind of line," Aiden quipped, and Zac couldn't not laugh at that.

"You're right. But I'm sorry if I've seemed moody tonight. The man from the admin offices I mentioned is my ex-husband. We split up over a year ago, but some days, it just doesn't feel that long to me. There are still times when I get thrown off without expecting it, and I think that's because I had to start my life over after we ended things. Sometimes, I feel like this still isn't my life at all, you know?"

"I think I do, yeah," Aiden said. "You want to talk about what happened? I'm here to listen, if that's what you need."

Zac grimaced. "You're nice to offer. And sure, I'll share some of the gory details—it's the least I can do after behaving the way I have—but not here with your friends." He reached for the doorknob. "Talking about my divorce would be the opposite of positive energy, and I'm not going to be responsible for casting a curse on your friends' show."

So Zac and Aiden found a corner in the living room and spent time talking with each other and Aiden's friends about theater and media and things that were *not* Zac's ex. That suited Zac just fine. Not until much later—after he and Aiden had ridden a Lyft to a diner in Chinatown where Aiden ate Dutch pancakes and Zac whole wheat toast with almond butter—did Zac open up a little about Edward and the life he'd thought they'd shared.

"So you were already working as a nurse practitioner when the two of you met?" Aiden said around a bite of pancake.

"Yes. I'd been at Mass. Eye & Ear for three years, and he'd just started applying to business schools." Zac pulled off his glasses and set them on the table. "Edward's five years younger than me."

"Dude, I'm not going to judge you for dating a younger man." Aiden nudged his plate of pancakes toward Zac and made pouty lips when Zac waved him off.

"Some people did judge us," he said. "Edward insisted the age difference didn't bother him though."

"Did it bother you?"

"Not at first. I was more concerned with my career getting in the way of my relationship than our age difference at the time. It can be hard for someone with a nine-to-five kind of job to be with a person who works the hours I do because my shifts are all over the map. Edward was adamant he could handle it though." Zac smiled. "That it didn't bother him and wouldn't going into the future. He's a very determined person—like one of those people who set a career path in fifth grade and never deviate—so I believed him."

"And you loved him?"

"Yes. He was an easy person to love. Dynamic and funny, and so smart. It sounds cliché to say he swept me off my feet, but that's how it felt. For the longest time, I couldn't believe he was interested in me at all."

Aiden frowned. "Why not?"

"Edward's very handsome. Really well put together too, and extremely charming. I'd never been out with anyone so attractive." *Until you,* Zac wanted to say, though of course, he didn't. He and Aiden were becoming friends, not dating. He cleared his throat. "Edward's one of those men who looks like he's stepped out of the pages of a magazine whereas I"—Zac glanced down at himself— "obviously don't."

"Zac?" Aiden cocked his head. "Are you under the impression you're not attractive?"

"I didn't say that."

"Yeah, you kind of did. And if you *were* under that impression, you'd be wrong."

Zac thought for sure his cheeks had caught fire. "Err, thank you. But you're misunderstanding me. And if you met Edward, you'd know what I was driving at. He did some modeling for a while when he was in school to make extra money. That's not something that would ever have happened to me." Zac smiled at Aiden's scoff.

"I was a chubby kid who grew into a not-so-skinny teen," he said. "Diabetes runs in the family on my father's side, and my mother worried. She was always trying to find the right mix of diet and exercise to get me down to a normal size, and I'm afraid she still does."

"There's no such thing as a normal size."

"I understand that now."

Aiden cocked his head. "Yeah?"

"Yeah." Zac sipped his coffee. "I like to think so, at least. I learned a lot about biology and nutrition when I started my nursing program, of course. I'd lost most of the bulk by then, but I have to work at staying this weight. Work hard, I might add, as in I should not be eating pasta from your truck."

"That can't be right." Aiden frowned. "Not eating pasta every day, fine, but never? Not possible unless you're literally unable. Besides, I think you look great. You're clearly fit but not too lean, which speaks to you being healthy and eating the right amount."

"Thank you, though I'm sure your idea of what constitutes the 'right amount' is very different from mine. I'd actually love it if I could eat less and still get by."

"That doesn't make sense," Aiden said, his voice gentle. "And hey, I cook for a living. I like the idea that the people in my life enjoy the food I make."

"You already know I enjoy your food, maybe too much." Zac

hid a grin behind his coffee when Aiden looked skyward.

"Okay, I can tell I'm not going to win this argument, so let's talk about something else. How long were you and Edward married?"

"Ugh." Zac wrinkled his nose. "I'd rather not talk about my ex anymore. Can't we talk about movies or books or anything else that has nothing to do with me?"

"Sure, we can do that some time too," Aiden said, "but right now, I'm on a Zac Alvarez fact finding mission because I did a whole lot of talking about myself last night and tonight. Humor me?"

Zac stayed silent a moment. He hated talking about Edward with anyone, never mind someone he didn't know very well. Admitting to his failures and the way Edward had treated him always made Zac feel shitty and low. Like he had no hope of making anyone happy and should just quit thinking that, someday, maybe things could be different with another man. Because Zac's problem wasn't rooted in finding Mr. Right—it was rooted in *Zac* being Mr. Wrong.

Even so, Aiden's smile softened his resolve. Probably because Zac liked the idea of seeing Aiden again. Of being his friend.

"Okay, fine," he said. "Edward and I were together for fifteen years and married for eight. We bought a house out in Arlington and adopted a cat. And a condo in Provincetown for summer vacations."

"Damn. That sounds grown up. Nice, too."

"It was," Zac said, then frowned. "Or, I thought it was. I thought I had the life I wanted, but it didn't work out that way."

Sympathy made Aiden's eyes somber. "What happened?"

"He left me for someone," Zac said simply. "A mutual friend of ours in fact. It took me a long time to understand something was wrong. Or to acknowledge it really. Because while I thought our relationship seemed off, it wasn't to the extent where I'd imagine my husband fucking around for six months before I caught on."

"Christ," Aiden grumbled. "What an asshole."

Zac made a "and there you go" kind of motion with his hand. "See why I don't like talking about it? But, honestly, I ignored some signs. Dismissed things I shouldn't have because I didn't want to believe either of them would actually hurt me like that."

"I'm sorry," Aiden said. The serious set of his features told Zac he meant it.

"Thanks. It was a challenge getting back on track, and it seemed to take forever, but I'm okay. And ... getting better lately. I used some of my share of the properties sales to buy an apartment here in the city and being back in Boston has been wonderful. Plus, I figured out which people in my life were real friends to me too. So, here I am." He met Aiden's gaze head on. "Turning forty-five this year and on my own for the first time in a long while."

Aiden didn't miss a beat. "Living the dream," he said with a grin that Zac immediately returned.

"Starting over. Accepting the rare date, but mostly working or staying in with the cat, so verging on hermit and social misfit."

Aiden snorted. "Please. You're not a proper social misfit until you've hung out with theater geeks and cooking nerds. Oh, which you've now done. You're fucked, dude."

As they laughed, Zac understood once more how much he'd missed such easy and simple human interactions. It felt good to talk and enjoy the art of being not very serious for a few hours.

"You don't have to wait with me," he said to Aiden as they exited the diner. "The car should be here in a minute."

"I know I don't have to wait." Aiden slid his hands in his pockets. "I want to though. I like talking to you."

"I like it too." Zac's stomach gave a giddy little flip. "What about you? Do you need a Lyft too, or are you taking the subway?"

"Oh, I'll probably walk." Aiden tipped his chin northward. "I live over in Fort Point, and it's a nice night for a walk over the bridge."

"Really?" Zac tried not to let his doubt show. "It's late, Aiden."

"And still safe. These neighborhoods are busy, and there're always lots of people out at this hour because the bars are still open."

Aiden fell quiet, his gaze on Zac, then pulled a hand from his pocket. He stepped closer and took hold of Zac's fingers, his voice softer when he spoke again.

"I'd like to see you again, Zac."

"Why?" Zac huffed a laugh at the face Aiden pulled.

"Dude, come on."

"I'm so sorry," Zac said. "That was rude."

"And yet, oddly, I'm still interested in you."

Zac cocked an eyebrow. "Interested?"

"Is that so hard to believe?" Aiden chuckled as Zac took a turn making a face. "Seriously, I had a good time last night and tonight, even with the bumps in the road. What do you say we do it again and see what happens?"

Zac opened his mouth, intent on telling Aiden he was mistaken. That he couldn't possibly be interested in a man fifteen years his senior, particularly one who'd just unloaded about a failed relationship over whole wheat toast. Before he could say any of those words however, Aiden gave Zac the sweet, open smile he liked so much. It made the doubts in Zac's head fade and warmed him through, so when he did finally speak, the words that came out weren't what he'd planned to say at all.

"Okay. I'd like that."

Aiden smiled wider, so his eyes crinkled at the corners, and quickly dropped a kiss on Zac's cheek. "Great. Oh, here's your car."

A pleasant buzz settled over Zac as Aiden tucked him into the Lyft, and it lingered long after he'd gotten back home. Even as he lay in bed waiting for sleep, Zac imagined his skin tingled with the memory of that kiss, and every time he thought about the shine in Aiden's eyes, Zac had to smile too.

Chapter Five

Getting to know Aiden became almost effortless after the ups and downs of those first two evenings. Zac sometimes wondered at how easily things fell into place, but then Aiden had a way about him that made everything very simple.

Zac stopped by the food truck whenever he was on shift, and though he didn't (couldn't) buy food every time, Aiden always insisted on slipping him a treat, whether it was cookies or fresh bread, or even hand-rolled truffles wrapped in brightly colored foil.

"Damn you for bringing these," Zac said as he bit into one of the dark chocolate spheres. It was the afternoon before Thanksgiving and Aiden had stepped out of the truck for a quick break so he and Zac could visit one of the neighboring trucks for cups of coffee to go with the chocolates. The truffles were infused with more exotic flavors than Zac would have expected, like saffron, matcha, and five-spice powder, and he hummed now as an irresistible mix of dark chocolate and wasabi hit his tongue. "Do you buy them locally?"

Aiden sniffed. "I think you know me better than that by now," he said.

Zac stared at the half-eaten treat between his fingers. "You made these?"

"I did indeed."

"They're so good, Aiden!"

"I know, right? Em and I are taking a chocolate-making class," Aiden said. "He wants to make up a box of truffles to give to Sean for Hanukkah, and I always like learning new things." He sipped from his cup, then shrugged. "Plus, the leftovers are a huge bonus. You're the only person I've shared them with."

"Now I feel special." Zac sucked a smudge of ganache from his thumb. "Even if eating them means yogurt for dinner."

Aiden balked. "Hey, no. I didn't give you those so you'd skip eating, Zac. You'll be working all night and you know yogurt's not going to be enough."

"Some nights, I'm thankful if I have time for anything, let alone yogurt." Zac reached over and squeezed Aiden's elbow. "Besides, I'm replacing a meal, not skipping altogether, and my metabolism will thank me for it later. Trust me when I say I'm not sad about making the sacrifice, by the way."

Zac changed the subject, and Aiden didn't mention it again, but Zac knew he wasn't happy about the yogurt-for-dinner plan. The message Aiden sent a few hours later said as much, too.

The antioxidants in dark chocolate are healthy, you know.

Zac smiled down at his phone. *In moderation, yes, they can be*, he replied.

And aren't 3 tiny truffles moderate?

I suppose so. Where are you going with this? Zac asked.

I'm going with you having a real meal for dinner, came Aiden's reply, quickly followed by another message. *So I left a salad for you at the nurse's station on floor 1.*

Zac stared at the words for several moments before he could reply. *Say what now?*

:D Trust me. It'll be good. Very in line with your healthy eating habits too. Tell me later if you like it.

Zac didn't doubt he'd like the salad, purely because Aiden had made it, and all the food Aiden made was outstanding. His insides went trembly as he headed for the nurse's station though. It'd been a very long time since someone had done something so thoughtful for him, and the feeling inside Zac mellowed into real pleasure as he collected a black cloth bag with a stainless-steel bento box packed inside.

You win, he wrote several hours later. It was nearly eight o'clock, and he'd practically inhaled the peppery arugula salad mixed with green kidney beans, lentils, and capers. His lips tingled pleasantly from a spice in the salty-sweet peanut sauce too, and if he hadn't been pleasantly full, he'd have eaten even more. *This dressing might just beat your vinaigrette. Plus this box is so fancy.*

I knew you'd like it, Aiden replied, and Zac could easily imagine his smirk. *I ate some too, and it kicked ass. I'm not usually one for lentils either.*

Zac chuckled softly. *You rocked your own world?*

Heck, yeah. Gonna feed the rest to Em tomorrow so he can share in the magic.

When the stars aligned and they both had the night off, Zac and Aiden met for dinner or a movie, sometimes with friends but more often alone, and they'd talk about whatever came up, as long as the topic was not Zac's divorce or his ex. Zac found himself agreeing to do all sorts of holiday-themed things when he and Aiden went out too—things he hadn't done in years like touring the many lighting displays around the city and ice-skating at the Frog Pond on the Boston Common.

"Is Zac short for Zachary?" Aiden asked one snowy evening. They'd been to the symphony that night for Handel's *Messiah* and afterward found a tiny Mediterranean restaurant on a side street for dinner. "Or were your parents just cool enough to give you a three-letter name?"

"My parents are cool but nowhere near that level," Zac replied. He bit into a stuffed grape leaf, then chewed and swallowed. "Zac is short for Zacarías, which comes from the Hebrew 'Zechariah.' It means 'The Lord has remembered' and, as good Catholics, my parents liked that." He hid a smile at the intensity that entered Aiden's gaze. "What?"

"I'm not sure I've ever heard you trill your 'Rs' like that

before."

"I don't have much opportunity outside of work to use my Spanish."

"It's pretty hot, Zac."

"I'll remember if we ever go out for tapas."

Aiden smiled down at his chicken gyro. "I know I don't look the part, but my father was part Mexican. I only speak kitchen Spanish though," he said, a wistful note in his voice. "You said your parents live in the Dominican Republic, right?"

Zac could only blink at the rapid change of topic. "I—yes, that's right," he said. "We lived in Baltimore while I was growing up, but they moved back to the D.R. after my dad retired. My sister and I helped them buy a villa on a golf resort in a city called La Romana. Mom and Dad love it, and we kids always have a place to vacation. Of course, neither Noemi nor I actually *go* on vacation so I'm not sure how much we're getting out of that end of the deal."

"Well, that's silly." Aiden fixed Zac with a puzzled look. "What the heck is wrong with the two of you?"

"Says the workaholic who never takes more than one day off at a time."

Aiden tipped his head back and cackled. "Damn, I need some burn cream after that one."

"Yeah, you do. You're not wrong though." Zac sipped his water. "The last time Noemi and I got down there together was over the summer, and that was to celebrate my father's birthday. Noemi's a nurse too, at Johns Hopkins back in Baltimore."

"I've only ever been there for work, but it seems like a fun city."

"It is, and my sister loves it. Thinks I'm nuts staying here with the snow and long winters."

"Lady's got a point. However, I'm not sure I'd know what to do at Christmas if I could wear shorts without fear of losing *my* nuts to frostbite."

Zac clapped a hand over his eyes and listened to Aiden snicker.

So many of their conversations were like that: meandering and light and filled with banter that Zac enjoyed immensely. Still, heavier topics did come up now and then because while Zac was clear about where his boundaries lay, Aiden seemed to have almost none and never hesitated to answer anything Zac asked.

"How old were you when you got your first tattoo, Aiden?"

They'd met up after Zac's shift that afternoon and done some gift shopping on Beacon Hill, then stopped for sushi at a place near Zac's apartment he'd never even been inside.

"Eighteen." Aiden slid his shirtsleeve up to expose the ink designs. "I'd started *planning* before then, but the Marinellis asked that I wait until I was legally an adult to start getting inked. I had to save up the money too."

"The Marinellis are Gianna's parents?"

"Yep. Carlo and Angelina, also known as Pops and Mamma. Angelina is—or was, I guess—my mother's second cousin."

"Gianna and her parents are actually blood family to you?" Zac smiled. "I didn't realize that. How fortunate you ended up with them."

"Absolutely."

"You know, before you told me you were adopted, I wondered how you got an Irish name with a sister named Gianna."

Aiden nodded. "You wouldn't be the first. When I was a kid, I thought about changing my name to Anthony so I'd fit into their Italian-ness better. Pops told me to keep my name though because he knew I'd appreciate it more as I got older. He was right of course."

"Did you mind that you took their surname?"

"Not at all. I took Daugherty as my middle name after James, so it was always close. Aiden James Daugherty Marinelli is a hell of a mouthful though, and fuck learning how to spell it." He dredged a piece of maki in soy sauce. "I briefly flirted with the idea of using Daugherty as my professional name after I decided to start up the business, but Marinelli has been my last name for so long I'd feel a bit weird answering to anything else.

"The knife is a nod to my profession, of course." He tucked the sushi roll in his mouth, then ran a thumb over the shape etched in bold black lines above his elbow. His wink was playful, but Zac knew the short sentences etched above and below the knife were words Aiden took to heart: *Live to cook. Cook to live.*

"Was it the first?" Zac pushed his glasses up his nose a bit.

"No. The Bodhi tree was first." Aiden pointed at an elegant tree drawn above the knife in the center of his deltoid muscle. "It's in memory of my parents, Thomas and Kathleen. I was only six when they died. I was also exploring Buddhism at the time I planned this tattoo and feeling very Tree of Life at the time." His expression grew more thoughtful as he moved his fingers over a compass drawn higher onto his shoulder.

"This one is for Pops and Mamma. They took me in and gave me a good life. Made me feel loved. They're the ones who taught me to cook, you know. And the compass is a symbol of how they helped me find my way when I needed it."

He paused, his long lashes hiding his eyes, and Zac's heart squeezed, both for Aiden's loss and the family he'd gained.

"The others are things I like or mark places I've visited that mean something to me," Aiden went on. His eyes were clear when he met Zac's gaze. He indicated a stylized flower in a shield. "This is a Florentine lily or Giglio. Florence was where I first truly understood how much food influences my outlook on life. We went there many times when I was growing up."

Next, he tapped a symbol formed by three interlocked spirals. "The Triskelion I got in Dublin. It stands for eternal life and a joining of balance, harmony, and continual motion." Aiden grinned. "I must have been going through a very existential time when I got that one too because it followed not long after the Bodhi tree. So many deep thoughts."

Zac had to laugh. "And the dog?" He pointed at what appeared to be a white bull terrier drawn so that it was sitting atop a car tire.

"Oh, that's Ripper. He was my first and still favorite dog." Aiden rubbed the dog's head with one finger. "He refused to sleep with anyone else but me, so I guess I was his favorite too."

43

"I love it." Zac folded his hands on top of the table to keep himself from touching Aiden's skin himself. "What about the other arm? Will you get inked there too?"

"Sure, eventually. I'm saving that arm for what happens next in my life. For when I have my own family and new memories and experiences." Something flashed in Aiden's eyes, too quick for Zac to read, and then he tipped his head at Zac's empty plate. "You ready for the check? Or can I maybe tempt you to split a coffee jelly with me?"

"What on earth is a coffee jelly? Do I even want to know?"

Aiden's eyes went round. "You've never had it? Oh, my God, we have to remedy that situation right now. It's coffee-flavored Jell-O drowning in sweetened cream. And, yes, you are going to have some cream." He narrowed his eyes the second Zac opened his mouth to protest. "You skipped out on booze with dinner, so I think you've got a little wiggle room on the caloric intake list in your head."

"I can't believe you used the world 'wiggle' in reference to a gelatin dessert." He smiled at Aiden's snicker. "But I don't need to eat anything else. That list is in my head for a reason, Aiden. I literally can't eat the way you do and stay this size."

"Okay, but …" Aiden paused for several beats.

"What is it?"

"I don't know. I guess we have different ideas about how much being 'the right size' matters." Zac could hear the air quotes in Aiden's voice, and a frown crossed Aiden's face as he continued speaking. "If I gained five, ten, twenty pounds, would you find me less attractive? Like me less?"

Zac's stomach fell clear down to the floor. "God, no. That wouldn't matter to me at all."

"I figured." Aiden's frown softened. "I hope you know I'd be the same, Zac. I like *you*, not your pants size. Okay?"

"Okay."

Aiden sighed. "Why do I feel like you don't believe me?"

"I guess … I'm pretty sure this is going to make you mad but being with you sometimes gives me déjà vu about my ex." Zac held up a hand when Aiden made an outraged noise. "Meaning that I wonder why you're interested in me at all. You're sort of famous around this town, Aiden, and I'm—"

"Someone I like and admire," Aiden said, his voice rich with conviction. "You have an advanced nursing degree, for crying out loud, Zac, which means your brain works in a thousand different ways mine never could. You help save people's lives every day and look freaking fantastic doing it, and every time we get together, I smile so much my face aches by the time I go home."

Heat crawled up the back of Zac's neck, but he smiled when Aiden reached over the table and took his hand. "I like you too."

"Good."

Aiden gave Zac's fingers a squeeze, then turned his attention back to ordering their dessert. Zac continued turning Aiden's words over in his head however, a quiet warmth running through him the whole time. No one had ever said anything like that to Zac before. Made him feel truly *seen* and in the very best way. And Zac's delight as he and Aiden shared the sweet, wiggly coffee jelly was genuine and deep, and made him feel lighter than he had in a long time.

After dinner, Aiden walked Zac home and, as he always did after they'd been out, kissed Zac just once. His lips met Zac's with the perfect amount of heat and lingered for a moment before he pulled away. Zac read a desire for more than that single kiss in Aiden's eyes as he said goodnight. And it was becoming more and more difficult for Zac to tear himself away too.

You appreciate Aiden's consideration, Zac reminded himself as he closed his apartment door. They'd talked about Zac's need to set a slower pace and how, even after over a year, he was still recovering from the fallout of his divorce. Zac wasn't even sure he was ready for something beyond flirting. The difference in age between Aiden and himself worried Zac too because if Edward had found Zac's life stifling with five years separating them, then surely fifteen was much, much worse.

Still … Zac found himself imagining things. Like feeling Aiden's long arms wrapped around him. Sliding his fingers through Aiden's unruly brown hair. The rasp of Aiden's stubble against Zac's cheek, and the way his mouth would taste. Zac liked Aiden a lot. He liked the way he felt when they were together even more, as if he'd finally started waking up after the long period of numbness that had followed Edward's betrayal.

Which is why Zac also found himself imagining what would happen if Aiden didn't stop at one kiss.

OoOoO

A few days later, Aiden didn't stop. They'd been ice skating at the Boston Common, then gone out to eat salted spiced squid and noodles at a restaurant in Chinatown. After a minute of lip nibbling, Aiden asked Zac to come to his apartment for a drink, and the mix of pleasure and surprise on his face when Zac agreed made Zac's insides twist with guilt.

"Don't look so surprised."

"I'm not! Okay, I am," Aiden chuckled. "I also know you're working tomorrow, so I figured I had a fifty-fifty shot."

"You're working tomorrow too," Zac pointed out. "Not to mention getting up at stupid o'clock to prep for a day full of cooking."

"That's my favorite kind of day," Aiden replied, his expression completely earnest. "I didn't work two night shifts this week like you did though. I'm surprised you're still standing, never mind capable of speech."

"Meh, you get used to it."

Aiden threaded his fingers through Zac's as they walked to his place in the Fort Point district. They'd held hands before of course, but only for a moment when they kissed each other goodnight. This was the first time Aiden had taken Zac's hand simply to hold, and while Zac told himself it wasn't any big deal, it felt like one.

The renovated factory where Aiden lived was on Melcher Street and boasted loft spaces filled with old brick and original wood beam ceilings. The grays and whites of the decor blended beautifully with the apartment's clean lines, even in the bathroom where Zac paused to splash water on his face and get ahold of his nerves. Once he'd emerged, he found Aiden in the kitchen that adjoined the open sitting area, pouring glasses of wine under strings of white fairy lights that hung over the open air of the loft and filled it with a soft white glow.

"Are these for Christmas?" Zac asked. "Or do you keep them up year-round?"

"I might after this year," Aiden said. "They were supposed to be up just for the winter holidays, but it took Em and Sean and me forever to string them up, so I'm very much tempted to leave them. Besides, I like the way they look. I'm going to put up a tree this week."

"It'll be beautiful, I'm sure. And wow, this view." Zac whistled low and walked toward a wall of enormous windows that looked out onto the Fort Point Channel itself. "This is gorgeous, Aiden."

"Thank you," Aiden said. "I love it here."

"Is there another room or do you sleep hanging upside down in the closet?"

"I spent too long mattress shopping not to use a bed."

Zac glanced back at Aiden, who turned and pointed to a staircase behind him. Following it with his gaze, Zac saw that it led to a second level over the kitchen. When he looked up, he could just see the bedroom over the edge of the balcony.

"Aha."

"Pops and Mamma helped Gianna buy this place back before the Seaport District was a thing and the whole neighborhood exploded." Aiden set the wine bottle on the counter. "After Gianna and Gerrit were married, I bought her out for a very, very reasonable price, and I've been here ever since. Sometimes, I think it might be nice to get away from the city and have a yard. Then I remember how much I hate mowing grass."

Zac pulled his glasses off with a hum and slipped them into his pocket. "Yard work is overrated."

His smile faltered as he remembered how proud Edward had been of the gardens and lawns of the homes he'd shared with Zac and, always observant, Aiden crossed the room toward him. He raised a hand to Zac's cheek.

"I poured you a glass," he murmured and went still when Zac shook his head.

"I don't need any wine."

Zac held his breath. He lifted a hand to cover Aiden's fingers resting on his face, and his heart beat wildly, blood rushing in his ears. Aiden licked his lips before he leaned in and brushed his lips against Zac's, and this time, he didn't back off. He lingered another beat instead, and the sweet pressure of his mouth made Zac feel flushed all over.

Zac closed his eyes. Cupping Zac's jaw, Aiden brought the other hand up and stroked his thumbs over Zac's cheekbones and beard, those touches electric. Grasping Aiden's waist, Zac let him in more, their mouths moving together as they learned each other's tastes.

Zac's breath hitched as Aiden ran his tongue over Zac's lips. A soft groan rumbling in his chest, Zac opened for him, and the warmth inside him burned hotter. He splayed his hands across Aiden's lower back and pulled him close, and Aiden hummed as their hips met.

Zac shivered, breathing a little harder when Aiden broke the kiss only to move his lips along the line of Zac's jaw. "God, Aiden, you feel so good."

"You do too," Aiden whispered between kisses. He crowded Zac against the window, his kisses growing hungrier. "I've wanted to kiss you like this for such a long time, you have no idea."

Somehow, he guided Zac to the sofa without their lips ever parting. The second Zac was seated, Aiden climbed onto his lap, knees pressed against Zac's hips and his arms around Zac's shoulders so their chests met. Zac's whole body burned.

He rubbed his hands over Aiden's back and arms, craving that contact, and couldn't remember when he'd last felt so good. It had been too long since he'd been touched like this. Made to feel desired. And all he knew now was that he wanted more.

His bones turned liquid as Aiden rolled his hips. Craning up to meet Aiden, Zac groaned low in his throat as Aiden sank his fingers into Zac's hair. Together, they shifted until Zac lay flat with Aiden over him, and Aiden swore when their cocks connected through their clothes. Zac's head spun at the sensation of Aiden hard and straining through his jeans.

He wants this as much as you do.

"Shit." Zac's voice was hoarse when Aiden pulled away, and he knew his grip on Aiden's shoulders was too tight.

Aiden merely pressed his forehead to Zac's, his breaths hot and fast over Zac's lips and his gaze heated. "This is okay, right? We can stop if you don't want this, or slow down—"

Zac rushed to cut Aiden off. "I don't want to slow down. I want this. Want you. Just don't stop touching me, Aiden, please."

"I won't." Aiden pulled back, fresh lust filtering over his features. He smoothed Zac's hair off his forehead, and there was awe in his voice when he spoke again. "Fuck, you're gorgeous. And you have no idea, do you?"

Zac had the presence of mind to chuckle, even though Aiden's words made him want to preen. "You're the gorgeous one."

A fleeting smile curved Aiden's mouth. He dropped his hand and slid it between them, palming Zac's cock, his touch delicious and rough. Zac's body reacted at once, hips bucking without his permission as a strangled noise filled his throat.

"Oh, fuck." Aiden's voice was gruff. "I want you so badly. Can I take you upstairs?"

Too lust-drunk to speak, Zac made an affirmative noise and forced himself to turn Aiden loose. Aiden climbed off Zac's lap and stood, one hand out to help Zac up.

Fuck, this is really happening.

They climbed the stairs in silence, hands entwined, and the moment they reached the top, Aiden turned and reached for Zac.

Their mouths connected in a wet crash of teeth and tongues that made Zac's knees wobble, and he almost staggered as Aiden drew him toward the bed.

Motions urgent, they pulled at each other's clothes, but Zac's breath caught after he'd gotten Aiden's Henley off. He stared, understanding only now that the tattoos in the half-sleeve extended onto Aiden's chest. They covered most of his right pectoral muscle with graceful black lines depicting angels, stars, and roses around an old-fashioned pocket watch and a quote drawn in graceful script letters.

Time moves in one direction, memory in another.

A pang shot through Zac's heart. "Beautiful," he murmured. He traced the tattoos with his fingers, the desire inside him coiling tighter at the sight of Aiden's skin pebbling under his touch. Aiden groaned when Zac grazed his nipple with one thumb, and the sound sent a bolt of lust right through Zac's core.

They sank onto the edge of the bed, kisses fevered, and Zac laid back, his hands on Aiden's ribs and guiding Aiden over him. Tracing a hot line along Zac's throat with his tongue, Aiden sucked and nuzzled, lapping at Zac's nipples until Zac hissed. He stroked Zac through his boxers even as he moved lower and dragged his tongue over Zac's belly, lavishing the muscles and soft skin with attention until Zac was so overloaded with sensation his body shook.

"Fuck, Aiden."

"Mmm, this body." Aiden sat back a bit, his cheeks flushed and his lips swollen. "You want more?"

"Jesus, yeah." Zac moaned. "I'm clear," he said. "Haven't been with anyone since—"

Aiden kissed the name Zac had been about to speak right off his lips. "I know. I'm negative too, in case you were wondering."

"Keep going," Zac rushed out. "I want to feel you."

"I want that too," Aiden murmured. He kissed Zac again, pushing his tongue deep as they held each other tight. Both were breathing hard by the time Aiden pulled away again.

Aiden got to his knees. He reached for the nightstand while Zac scooted higher on the mattress, and Zac grinned when a bottle of lube landed near his knees. Aiden's eyes were gleaming when Zac met his gaze.

"I love this," Aiden said, his voice rich with pleasure. "It's been a while since I unwrapped a beautiful man in this bed." Hooking his thumbs under Zac's waistband, he dragged the boxers slowly down over Zac's groin and kissed the tender skin there until Zac cursed him for being too goddamned slow.

A growly laugh came out of Aiden. He urged Zac to lift his hips, then drew the boxers the rest of the way down Zac's legs and set them aside before he turned his attention to stripping himself off. Zac fisted the sheets, so hard he ached as Aiden settled onto the bed again, his own cock red and rigid against his abdomen.

Aiden made a show of slicking his hands with lube, but Zac still jumped slightly at his touch. Cupping Zac's balls in one hand, Aiden massaged the tender skin with slow, maddening circles.

"This okay?" he asked, voice breathless as he teased his fingers into the cleft of Zac's ass. "You like this, Zac?"

"Yeah." Zac could hardly catch his breath. He needed so badly to be filled, to feel that spiral of razor-edged pleasure, to soar and crash wherever Aiden wanted to take him. "Like it. Need it."

"Okay. I'll make you feel good, Zac." There was promise in Aiden's voice and fire in his gaze as he stared Zac down.

Now Zac could only nod. He trusted Aiden to be good to him. He let his knees fall open, heart pounding as Aiden teased him some more, his touches driving Zac higher and higher until a finger finally pushed inside him.

"Oh, fu-u-u-ck," he said on a groan. The rush of sensation that coiled down Zac's spine nearly stole his breath.

Aiden's erection pressed hot and hard against Zac's thigh, but before he could think to reach for him, Aiden had slid a second finger home, and Zac melted even more into the mattress. A weak curse on his lips, he surrendered completely as Aiden bent to take Zac between his lips, that heat turning every rational thought in

Zac's brain to ash. He gasped and writhed and wound his fingers tightly in Aiden's hair, his skin so hot he thought he might burst. Aiden took him deep and moaned like he loved it each time Zac thrust up.

"Shit," Zac got out. "Need to come, Aiden. I—oh, *fuck*."

A roar building in his ears, Zac forced his eyes open so he could stare down at the man between his legs, and his whole chest squeezed tight as their gazes met. Aiden's eyes were glassy, and his lips stretched wide as he sucked, his lids fluttering when Zac pulled his hair. Then Aiden curled his fingers inside Zac, and Zac's pleasure imploded.

He came so hard he could hardly breathe. Zac flew high, his own voice muted in his ears, with only Aiden's touch to ground him as he slowly, slowly floated back down. Aiden was on top of Zac when he came back to himself, his weight solid between Zac's legs.

He rocked against Zac, lips hot as he pressed kisses onto Zac's throat, and Zac felt him then, his cock like steel against Zac's thigh. Zac kissed Aiden, his skin prickling at Aiden's desperate noise and the taste of himself on Aiden's tongue. Zac reached for Aiden's cock and relished the way Aiden shivered when Zac ran his thumb over the head.

"So good," Aiden murmured, his eyes mere slits when Zac pulled back. He humped into Zac's fist, his babbling words like a mantra as Zac gathered him close. "You make me feel so good. So good, Zac. I need—oh-h-h. Need to come."

"I know." Zac angled their bodies together, tightening his grip when Aiden gasped. "Come on me, Aiden. Let me feel you."

Aiden curled into Zac only moments later, his voice shaking and his body pliant as his cock pulsed hot and wet between them.

Oh, baby.

Zac swallowed down those words. They lay together a long time in the aftermath, swapping drowsy kisses until Aiden finally roused himself enough to grab his discarded shirt. He wiped them both clean, then tossed the shirt toward the bathroom and wound himself around Zac again.

"That's kind of a frat boy move," he said, "but I'm too zonked to do much more."

Zac set his head on Aiden's chest. "I'm not going to judge you. My legs are made of rubber right now, and I'd probably fall if I tried to get up right now."

"So stay." Aiden moved his lips against Zac's hair, his hold growing a little tighter, as if he thought Zac might bolt. "I know you're on duty tomorrow, and I'll be awake by five. Will your cat be okay?"

"I fed him before I left to meet you."

"Sweet. Then I'll make sure you're up in the morning before I have to leave."

"Sounds promising," Zac said and smiled at Aiden's soft laughter. Still, he tilted his head back so he could see Aiden's expression. "You don't mind?"

"Of course not." Aiden's lips turned up on one side, his eyes sleepy as he stared down at Zac. "Your being here is the last thing I'd mind, Zac. Stay."

He kissed Zac some more, deep and sweet, and warmth unfurled inside Zac. He set his ear against Aiden's chest again and listened to the thump-thump of his heart and the way Aiden's breaths evened out as Zac followed him into sleep.

Chapter Six

Mark smiled wide as he opened the brown takeout box Zac had set in front of him. "Thank you."

"You're welcome. What's with the face?" Zac turned his attention to the kidney bean and lentil salad he'd ordered in lieu of pasta. "You look like the proverbial cat that ate the canary."

"You mean ate the cacciatore." Mark smirked at Zac's groan. "You stepped right into that one, man. As in literally *gave* me a container of cacciatore, for crying out loud."

"Okay, fine, I did. Doesn't explain your smirky smug ways, though."

Mark shrugged. "Maybe I feel smug seeing you like this."

"Like what?"

"Smiling. Happier." Mark's smirk softened. "You look good, Zac. Better."

"Oh." Zac could feel his ears turning red. "Better than what?"

"Than you have in a while." Mark paused and licked his lips. "After things ended with Edward, you withdrew from everything."

Zac said nothing. Mark was right—Zac had retreated from the world when his marriage had dissolved. It was how he'd coped with his life having fallen to pieces.

"I get why you did it," Mark said. "Or, I think I do anyway. From the little you've said, it sounds like Edward put you through a lot. I can't imagine how hard it must have been on you."

"It sucked. Getting through even a good day felt … impossible. Like even bothering to wake up every morning was pointless." Zac shook his head. "That probably sounds very dramatic."

"It doesn't." Mark frowned. "I wish we'd known how to make it better for you."

Zac ached at the regret he glimpsed in Mark's eyes. They'd been friendly before his divorce but gotten a lot closer since, mostly because Mark had decided he'd force his friendship on Zac no matter what. For all his joking and rakish playacting, Mark rarely said things he didn't mean. Zac hoped he would never have to see his friend hurt the way he had or endure the same kind of scars.

"I'm not sure anyone could have made it better." Zac managed a tight smile. "People *were* there for me, though—you, our friends, my family. And that made it easier to get through the days when I needed it."

"Good. You've been coming back these last few weeks." Mark's gaze turned appraising, but it was still kind. "You're more like the guy I used to know before you got divorced. And I'm guessing that's got a lot to do with a certain food truck owner."

"Why would you say that?"

"Gee, I dunno, Zac. Maybe because Aiden put a salad he invented for you on the truck's menu? If that doesn't tell you the boy's got hearty eyes for you, I'm not sure what will."

Zac's laugh put Mark's smirk firmly back into place. "Okay, yes. Aiden's been great."

"So busted," Mark muttered. "Still a nice change seeing you this way."

Zac thought it was a nice change too.

OoOoO

Aiden's catering schedule got busier as the countdown to Christmas and New Year's continued. He still spent as much time as he could with Zac and cooked when they spent time at his place, which now boasted a tree covered in twinkling lights that matched the ones hanging over the loft. Aiden introduced Zac to some of his favorite dishes, and learned some of Zac's, and always tweaked them just enough so Zac could actually eat without beating himself up (much) afterward. Some evenings they worked together on Aiden's sofa, decorating the glassine paper bags with hand-drawn snowflakes and snowmen while they gossiped about Zac's patient load or the romantic dramas among members of Endless Pastabilities' crews. Other times they met up with friends and mixed their circles together, so Em and Sean got to know Mark and Owen, and they all gathered for a game night at Jace and Paul's. Every night Zac and Aiden met, they ended up at Aiden's loft where they learned the ways of pleasuring one another.

Occasionally, Aiden suggested they go to Zac's apartment, but Zac always found a way to shut him down, even when going to his place would have been easier for them both. Zac felt shitty doing it too, especially in the moments when he caught a mix of confusion and hurt flash over Aiden's face. Zac couldn't stop himself though. He didn't want to either because, as far as he'd come, a part of him still needed to hold some things back from Aiden—keep the deepest parts of himself safe—even when doing so caused them pain.

"I feel bad that you've effectively orphaned your cat," Aiden said one evening as they were cleaning up after dinner.

"You really don't need to." Zac set the plate he'd just rinsed into Aiden's dishwasher. "My neighbor takes him next door when I call to let her know I won't be home. Besides, I'm not sure Gordon even misses me."

Aiden paused in the act of moving leftovers into another of the steel bento boxes he kept around. "Gordon? That's your cat's name?"

"Yes. He was my ex's cat. I'm more of a dog person and didn't want a cat at all."

"But you took him in anyway?"

"I didn't have much of a choice." Zac turned off the faucet and reached for a dishtowel. "My ex couldn't take Gordon, so he stayed with me." Drying his hands, Zac showed Aiden a weak smile. That sounded a lot better than explaining that Edward's boyfriend had told Zac he'd rather turn the cat over to a shelter than keep him. Zac'd never told anyone about that conversation. Not even Edward. "Turns out a cat's not bad company," he said. "We're two old guys with graying hair who like to watch TV and veg out on the couch, so it's a good match."

Zac's joke fell flat because his voice had gone wrong and stiff again, and he could see the effect it had on Aiden in the way he pressed his lips into a grim line.

"You could …" Aiden flicked his gaze around the loft. "Would it be weird to bring Gordon over here sometimes? I mean, there's plenty of space, and that way he'd still get to hang with you. The tree might be a problem, but maybe we could put up a barrier."

The hesitation in his voice and manner made Zac's chest tighten. It didn't match at all with the confidence that normally poured off Aiden, and it was almost painful seeing him so tentative. But before Zac could say anything—and gently shut down the idea of bringing Gordon to the loft—Aiden blinked, his expression startled, as if he'd remembered something that didn't make him happy.

"Holy shit, what am I even talking about?" Aiden gave a tight laugh and turned back to the leftovers. "Pay no attention to me, Zac. I'm tired and my brain got ahead of my mouth."

"It's fine," Zac murmured. "I appreciate the thought."

"Yeah, except dragging a cat across town is a terrible idea. I don't even know where that came from." Aiden tossed him a brighter than usual grin. "Hey, you mind if we talk about the menu I'm planning for a holiday party next Saturday? I want to run a couple ideas by you."

"Um, sure." Zac watched Aiden move toward the refrigerator with the box. "I'm not sure how much help I can be, but I'm always happy to listen. Who's throwing the party?"

"The doctors and nurses at Mass. Eye & Ear." Aiden waggled

his brows. "Gianna already told me you're off duty that night, and I want the food to kick extra levels of ass if you're planning to go."

"I hadn't decided." Though Zac had just now as pleasure swooped through him. His colleagues at the hospital teamed up every year to throw a holiday party in a function space that sat on the cusp of Zac's neighborhood. Provided he hadn't been on duty, Zac had nearly always found the parties fun, and knowing Aiden would be there this year made the evening sound even better. He slid his glasses higher onto his nose. "Why didn't you tell me you were doing the catering before now?"

"Clearly, someone hasn't checked the party invite," Aiden said, his voice lilting as he teased. "We catered the party last year too. Teamed up with another truck's team and basically each took a side of the room, which we'll be doing again this time around." He cut his gaze away again, his voice becoming quieter as he started gathering pans from the stove. "You were probably busy last year though."

Busy not falling apart because my life was in shambles, sure.

Zac swallowed the thought down. No need to bring up how raw he'd been last December. How he'd skipped the hospital's holiday party—along with every other holiday invite—in favor of holing up in his new apartment with the cat so he could watch TV until his eyes burned or he slept, whichever came first.

Zac didn't want to do that again. Especially not if Aiden was going to be there.

"I'm not busy *this* year," he said, "and I'd like to go." His words made Aiden throw him another grin. "So tell me about your ideas and what you'd like to cook."

Despite the easy conversation that followed, Zac thought Aiden seemed just the slightest bit off. Even as they tumbled into bed to watch TV, he'd been unusually quiet, and while they'd kissed and petted until they were drowsy and half-drunk with pleasure, his eyes had been somber. That kept Zac awake after Aiden had fallen asleep.

This kid could wreck you, the voice in Zac's head murmured, *and this time, you might not come back from it.*

The air around Zac went still as he argued with himself that Aiden would do no such thing. Yes, he had the power to hurt Zac, but so did nearly everyone Zac cared for. He didn't think Aiden would though, at least not on purpose. Aiden was different from so many men Zac knew, with his strange mix of maturity and lightheartedness, and intensely thoughtful in ways Zac had never expected. Zac didn't imagine Aiden had a mean bone in his body.

You thought the same about Edward.

As if he'd heard Zac's internal debate, Aiden murmured as he dreamed. A deep sleeper, he liked to sling an arm over Zac's waist and tangle their legs together, his breaths warm against the back of Zac's neck.

Zac turned over, his motions slow and careful so that Aiden slumbered on. His eyelids trembled and his breaths changed, and his full lips curved into a pout that Zac simply could not resist. Slowly, slowly he leaned in and kissed Aiden, sighing at the mix of softness and beard stubble as Aiden slowly stirred.

He grasped Zac tighter, breathing in deeply through his nose while Zac nuzzled him awake, and hummed as Zac slipped his tongue between Aiden's lips.

Heat pooled in Zac's groin. Aiden skated his fingers down Zac's torso, sliding them over his skin before he reached for Zac's boxers. He paused, teasing his fingertips under the waistband, then kissed Zac deeply, the wet slide of their tongues making Zac's heart race and his cock stir. He bit back a whimper as Aiden pulled away.

"Need you," Aiden told him, and Zac could only nod.

They wasted no time stripping each other bare, and a groan rolled through Zac as Aiden palmed Zac's cock. He wound his arms around Aiden's neck and basked in Aiden's greedy noises.

"Want you too," Zac managed between kisses, then shivered as Aiden turned his attention to Zac's neck. "Mmm, Aiden."

"Love the way you sound when we're like this," Aiden said, voice low. "Like you could come just from my hands on you."

"Fuck, I could. You have no idea what you do to me."

With a soft grunt, Zac pushed Aiden until he lay flat on the mattress. He lavished attention over Aiden's chest and belly, licking and sucking the tight muscles, desire snaking along his spine.

"*Zac.* Oh, my God."

Zac worked his way lower, running his teeth gently against Aiden's ribs, and smiled when Aiden barked out a laugh. Aiden brought a hand to rest against Zac's neck, and Zac let Aiden guide him back up until their lips met in a searing kiss. Sweat broke out over Zac's skin.

He gasped as Aiden flipped them and pinned Zac down with the weight of his body. Reaching between Zac's legs with one hand, Aiden tugged his balls, and the sting of pleasure pulled a whine out of Zac. He arched up against Aiden, heat racing under his skin.

"Need you," he managed, unashamed of the waver in his voice. "Inside me, now."

Aiden cupped Zac's cheek with his hand. "Okay, Zac. I've got you."

His words—the intent in his voice—tugged at Zac as Aiden kissed him again. But Aiden pulled away again, and Zac threw his arms over his head, his insides strung tight. Hearing the click of the lube bottle and the sound of tearing foil, his dick throbbed, and he spread his legs wide. Aiden was there in an instant, one hand trailing cool slick up the cleft of Zac's ass.

"Oh, God," Zac got out.

"Easy." Aiden used his other arm to cradle Zac, and Zac closed his eyes as Aiden slid a finger inside him.

"Yes," Zac whispered, his skin pebbling under the kiss Aiden dropped on his shoulder. He drew Aiden even closer and begged without shame until Aiden cursed and pulled his fingers free.

Zac was so far gone he could hardly focus by the time Aiden settled in between his legs. Aiden pressed forward, breaching the tight ring of muscle, pausing at Zac's sharp inhale before he slid into Zac in a long, slow push. Zac shoved his face into Aiden's throat, breathing through the stretch and burn.

"Okay, Zac?"

Heat slashed through Zac. He brought his arms up under Aiden's and hugged him tight, aware of Aiden trembling against him, his grip like iron around Zac's shoulders and waist.

"Yes," Zac hissed. Aiden rocked back and forward again, and the sharp ache in Zac's body changed, blooming into a pleasure that throbbed all through him. "Fuck, Aiden. *Fuck.*"

Aiden made a broken sound. He drove into Zac, their kisses open mouthed and messy as he reached between them and fisted Zac's cock. Zac started floating, time melting around him as they moved together, his breathless gasps loud in his own ears. Aiden pushed deep, scraping his cock against Zac's prostate, and Zac's whole body lit up. He shook and moaned in Aiden's arms, painting their bodies with his cum, and only then did Aiden let go.

He swore, thrusting hard until his movements stuttered, and when he came, his grip on Zac was almost too hard. But Zac reveled in the sting, just as he did in the way Aiden allowed Zac to wrap him up and hold him even tighter.

Chapter Seven

"Wow."

Zac stared at Aiden like he'd never seen him before. He'd known Aiden would be attending the party in chef mode, even though he wouldn't be cooking. Zac hadn't *understood* what that meant until he'd entered the function room just now and caught sight of Aiden, deep in discussion with Emmett and dressed in the formal uniform of black trousers and double-breasted black jacket. A jacket that set off Aiden's wide shoulders and narrow waist and gave him an added air of authority that made Zac's stomach flip.

"Zac!" Aiden handed the tablet he'd been holding to Emmett, who sent a cheery wave Zac's way, and crossed the room, his smile brighter than the holiday lights shining all around them.

"You look wonderful," Zac said.

"Yeah, and so do you," Aiden said. He walked up to Zac, admiration clear in his gaze. "Damn, you've been holding out on me. You're always hot, but I'd have figured out a way to get you into that suit ages ago if I'd known you look *this* fine!"

"Thank you." Zac leaned in for a quick kiss. "I'd argue that you look far more impressive, but I don't think you'd believe me. Why have I never seen you in a chef's uniform before?"

Aiden glanced down at himself. "Eh, because a T-shirt is a million times more practical when you're working on a food truck?

Besides, no one cares what I wear—they're all way more interested in how I cook. I'm not doing much of that tonight of course, but still"—he rubbed his hands together—"I want everything to go off without a hitch."

"It will." Fondness bloomed in Zac's gut. So typical of Aiden to ignore the fact that his handsome face and lean build were as big a draw as his food. Zac opened his mouth to say exactly that but closed it again when a trio of event planners appeared en masse, each exuding enough nervous energy to power a rocket and waving at Aiden.

"Uh-oh. That's my cue to go schmooze for a bit." Aiden wrinkled his nose. "I was hoping we'd have time to at least grab a drink before the circus started."

Zac squeezed Aiden's elbow. "Don't worry about it. We'll have time to catch up once the hungry masses have had a chance to eat."

He shooed Aiden off and turned his attention to the crowd, which was swelling larger every minute, and wanted to cheer when he spied Gianna and her husband headed his way.

"I'm seriously bummed Mark couldn't be here tonight," Gianna said over wine and hors d'oeuvres. "He insisted he wanted New Year's Eve off instead though, so I gladly traded him the time."

"He and Owen are flying out of town for New Year's," Zac replied. "I know there's sun and beach involved, which makes me think they're going to the Bahamas to visit Owen's parents. Sounds nice compared to the freezing temps we might get here."

Gianna cocked an eyebrow. "Well, now I don't feel bad at all. Especially since Aiden's here tonight doing his thang. These meatballs are so good!"

Gerrit snickered and plucked another from the plate he and Gianna had been sharing. "You say the same thing every time we eat them, you know. It's like we haven't tasted them a million times already."

"Well, I haven't gotten sick of them yet. Plus, I think my brother did something new to the sauce, so this *could* be the first time I'm tasting them." Gianna aimed a grin at Zac that quickly faded. "Tell me you're eating a few tonight, huh? In the spirit of Christmas?"

"Actually, no." Zac chuckled at Gianna's dramatic gasp. "I've been acting as Aiden's guinea pig for the last week, so I've had *more* than enough of my share of meatballs. I enjoyed every one too, just as I enjoy everything else he puts in front of me."

Gerrit held out a fist for Zac to bump. "Atta boy."

"You're right about the sauce, Gianna," Zac added. "Aiden dropped a scant teaspoon of saffron in just after the tomatoes, if I remember correctly."

"You absolutely do." The chef himself appeared beside Zac, his cheeks flushed from activity and his eyes sparkling with good humor. He accepted hugs from everyone as well as the glass of wine Zac had ordered him. "And listen to you, Zac, talking like you know your way around a kitchen!"

"Hah. Talking's still the only thing I'm comfortable doing in anyone's kitchen," Zac said. "God knows, I can hardly boil a pot of water without ruining the pot."

Aiden laid an arm over Zac's shoulders and smiled. "I know I could teach you if you'd just let me."

He cast his gaze around the ballroom, his eyes glowing as he watched the way people buzzed around the serving stations. He had no idea his words stung Zac though. They were another reminder of how Aiden wanted to share so much more than Zac felt ready to accept. Zac kept that to himself, however, and nodded as Gianna and Gerrit headed off to take another pass at the food tables.

"This was fun," Aiden said. "I think it's safe to say the food has been a big hit tonight."

"You say this like you're surprised." Zac kept his tone teasing.

"I'm not." Sipping his wine, Aiden scanned the room again. "I know how well my staff can cook and that our recipes are strong. I still wanted everything to go over well."

"You've said so a couple of times now. And everything did, of course." Zac tilted his head and watched Aiden, who looked suddenly shy. "Why were you worried?"

The tips of Aiden's ears turned red. "I wanted to impress you. Gianna and Gerrit too. You've never been to an event catered by my crew before, and I didn't want anything to go wrong."

This man.

Zac bit back a sigh. He wanted to say that Aiden impressed him almost daily with his skills, intelligence, and integrity. That Zac thought him fearless and bold but still wonderfully kind and lovely in too many ways to list. That Aiden made him feel alive after a long time of feeling empty. He didn't quite dare though.

He reached out and took Aiden's hand, threading their fingers together and swinging their joined hands gently. "I see."

"That probably makes me sound silly."

"Not at all. Though, I will point out that I've eaten your food dozens of times by now, and never once did I think it was anything less than wonderful."

Before Aiden could reply, one of the event planners was back and had a hand on his other arm.

"I'm so sorry to interrupt," she said, "but we've arranged for a few of the administrative staff to meet you and Keiko and your crews. We thought that'd make a nice photo op over by the cooking stations."

"And by 'cooking stations,' I'm guessing you mean 'kitchen.'" Aiden aimed a "what the fuck" face at Zac before he held out his glass. "Hang on to this, and I'll be right back."

"Of course." Zac couldn't hold back his smile as he watched Aiden stride off—the tailored black jacket did wonderful things to the figure he cut—which was why he missed the figure approaching on his left until it was too late to get away.

"Hello, Zac. Happy Holidays. Fancy meeting you here."

Zac stood frozen and staring into his ex-husband's gray-green eyes for several seconds. Inhaling deeply, he gave Edward a nod. "Merry Christmas, Edward. I didn't realize you'd be here tonight." He forced himself to smile. "You do know this is a party for doctors and nurses, right?"

Edward returned Zac's smile at once. "Oh, yes. The admin party isn't even until next week. Stanton desperately wanted to meet the chefs at *this* party though. He wrangled a couple of invitations out of one of the surgeons, someone he plays golf with on occasion. I did email and tell you I was coming, but I get the feeling you just ignore all of my messages."

"My bad." Zac's stomach twisted at Edward's mention of his boyfriend's name and tightened even more as a sudden thought occurred to him. "Where is Stanton now? Meeting the chefs?"

"Yes. I'm sure you remember what he's like about food and cooking—he'd much rather go out to eat than see a show. He's mad for the Marinelli boy *and* his food." Edward smirked. "I swear Stanton visits the store over near South Station at least three times a week. I keep telling him he needs to watch it with all that pasta or he's not going to fit into his clothes." His smile faded abruptly. "Sorry. That was bitchy."

"It's all right." Zac gave a half shrug. Edward had always been very conscious of Zac's dietary habits when they'd been together. Unfortunately, he'd been self-conscious and often defensive about his own love of food, which had sometimes made it difficult to enjoy eating together. "I've had the food from Endless Pastabilities, and it's wonderful."

"Isn't it? Doesn't hurt that everyone who cooks and works in those trucks and windows is exceptionally attractive. I'm surprised I've never seen you at the truck outside the hospital." Puzzlement crossed Edward's handsome features. "You know, I could have sworn that's who you were speaking to before I came over here. Aiden Marinelli, I mean."

"Oh, yes?" Zac said. He tried not to notice the flash of Edward's dimples.

"Yes. Though it seems unlikely, given the way you feel about food."

Zac blinked. "I like food. I just told you I've eaten from Endless Pastabilities. And you were right—I was talking to Aiden before you came over here."

Now Edward's brows rose. "How do you know him?"

"Know who? Hello, Zac. Happy Yule and all that."

Even now, that familiar voice made Zac's jaw clench. He bit the inside of his cheek as the man he used to call a friend joined them. "Stanton."

Stanton's gaze moved up and down Zac's body with an appraising gleam. "You look good. Really good. Even better, I daresay, than you did when you were with Edward. Wouldn't you agree, sweetheart?"

"There's no surprise in that." Edward frowned. "Zac always looks good."

"Oh, sure. I'm intrigued more than surprised and can't help assuming there is a 'who' who's put the spark back in Zac's pretty brown eyes." Stanton's expression turned coy. "Is that who you were talking about when I walked up?"

Zac'd never liked that bitchy edge Stanton seemed to revel in. No one was spared its sting, not even Edward himself, and it got under Zac's skin tonight as much as it had in the past. "Yes and no actually. Edward was asking me about Aiden Marinelli."

Stanton's eyes sparkled. "Oh, I met him!" The man appeared positively giddy as he shared a smile with Edward. "Just a minute ago in the kitchens. He and the crew were lovely, just as I imagined, though it was literally a handshake, snap a photo, and on your way."

"You'll be impossible now, I'm sure." Edward glanced back to Zac. "He'll be bragging about this for weeks. Probably won't wash his hand."

Stanton also turned his focus to Zac. "You know who we're talking about, don't you, Zac? I know food's not your thing, but I feel like you can't possibly have missed the food trucks outside of the hospital, and especially Endless Pastabilities. Edward says he sees it every day."

"Aiden cooks in that truck," Zac replied. "I met him there, actually. He's told me before that he feels he should spend more time in the Test Kitchen at Dewey Square, but he can't seem to tear himself away from cooking on four wheels." A mean kind of satisfaction streaked through him as he watched Edward's expression go blank and Stanton blink several times.

"You were saying a minute ago that you know him," Edward said, his words slow. "But not how."

"Well, as I said, we met at his truck. Aiden sold me some of the best pasta I've ever eaten." At that moment, a movement in the crowd caught Zac's eye, and he glanced over to see Aiden waving at him from the bar. He nodded when Aiden held up a finger in a sign that meant he'd be a bit longer.

"We're dating," Zac said, eyes still on Aiden. He tapped his wristwatch with his finger and smiled at Aiden's wink.

Stanton's brows were high on his forehead when Zac glanced at him again.

"You're seeing Aiden Marinelli?" Stanton asked.

"Yes."

"Holy shit." Stanton let out a harsh laugh. His mouth stretched wide, but the gleam in his eye was anything but happy. "What the hell are you thinking? That kid is almost young enough to be your *son*."

A hardness rose in Zac's chest and made his voice cold. "Don't be a drama queen."

"Am I?" Stanton scoffed. "He's practically a child."

"Aiden is thirty years old, Stanton. He's a grown man."

Stanton rolled his eyes. "Who doesn't recognize who he's dealing with clearly. Christ, Zac, I would have thought you'd have learned your lesson after your experience with Edward."

"And what lesson would that be?"

"That you should stick to what you know." Stanton pursed his lips. When he spoke again, his voice was quieter, almost earnest. "You need someone more like yourself. A homebody who likes things easy and quiet. Someone who is content watching the world go by instead of really experiencing it. There's no shame in that— there never was. But you with a guy like Aiden Marinelli doesn't make sense. Jesus, you run ten miles to burn off *salad*, never mind spaghetti. And you're unbearably naïve if you think that kid will stick around for even half as long as Edward did."

"Enough," Edward said quietly. His face was set in a deep frown that softened when he glanced back to Zac. "I'm sorry, Zac. I hope we haven't spoiled your evening."

"For Christ's sake, Ed—"

"No." Edward cut a quick glare at Stanton. "Giving Zac shit was not on my agenda tonight, and you knew that." At Stanton's huff, Edward turned back to Zac, and this time, he looked almost sad.

"Believe it or not, I'm glad I ran into you. And that you're doing well and look … great." He smiled then. "Have a nice Christmas, Zac. And maybe check your messages now and then, hm?"

Despite his ex's kind words, a cold numbness crept over Zac after Edward and Stanton had walked away. He sipped his wine and stared unseeing at nothing, pop music Christmas songs worming their way into his brain until a familiar voice cracked through the haze.

"Hey, sorry about that."

Zac blinked hard as Aiden appeared in front of him. "It's fine," he replied, his voice much steadier to his ears than he felt inside. "I know this is more than just a holiday party for you. You have a lot of commitments."

"Commitments I have fulfilled! Em said he'd handle everything from here on out, which means I am free and all yours." He rubbed his hands together. "Is that my glass of wine?"

"Yes, of course." Zac slid the glass Aiden's way, his heart tugging at the smile Aiden flashed.

"Thanks. As much fun as these evenings can be, it's nice when I can just be myself again." Aiden heaved a big breath and let it out. "Especially if I get a reprieve from the aftermath."

"Meaning clean up?"

"Clean up, pack up, and put away, yes—things my crew is incapable of doing quietly after a job." A chuckle rolled through Aiden. "They're talking about going for a drink as soon as this party is done. Sounded to me like a bar in South Boston will be their final destination."

Zac nodded numbly. "Do you need to go with them?"

"No." Aiden raised an eyebrow at Zac. "Unless you'd like to join them?"

"I don't think so, no. But you should go if you need to."

"My crew gets enough of me every damned day." Aiden laughed. "I'm happy to take you if you'd like to go though. I'll warn you now that it could be pretty raw—this crew and alcohol can be a potent mix. Definitely not your scene."

Those words sent an ache through Zac. "I told you before that I don't have a scene."

"Hey. What's wrong?" The smile slid off Aiden's face. "You look upset all of a sudden."

Zac shook his head. Stanton was right. He and Aiden didn't make sense. However genuine Aiden's feelings appeared to be right now, they were infatuation. They *couldn't* be anything but. And one day, they'd fade, and Aiden would be gone, just as Edward had gone before him. And the idea of how much that would hurt pushed Zac to run.

"I'm sorry," he muttered. "I should go. And you should be with your crew."

"What?" Aiden set his glass down. "What do you mean? If you want to leave, I'll come with you."

"No, you don't need to do that. I'll … I'll call you tomorrow, okay? We can talk then."

As badly as Zac wanted to turn around and leave, the increasing upset and confusion in Aiden's expression kept him rooted to the spot.

"I don't understand," Aiden said. "Did I say the wrong thing?"

"No." A familiar weariness fell over Zac. "I'm just tired and need to go home. Goodnight."

"I'll walk with you."

"Aiden—"

"Forget it." Something dark crossed Aiden's face as he took

Zac's elbow. "I'm walking with you, Zac, and you can just deal with it."

Silence hung over them as they retrieved their coats from the coat check and made their way out of the hotel, each step twisting the tension in Zac's middle even tighter. Every part of him wanted to touch Aiden, but he didn't dare, and the grim set of Aiden's mouth made it hard for Zac to breathe. Real dread filtered over him by the time his apartment building came into view, and he finally put a hand on Aiden's arm to keep him from walking any farther.

"Aiden, listen—"

"Just tell me what happened back there," Aiden broke in. "We were having a nice time, and I know I was busy tonight, but—"

"My ex was there." Zac dropped his hand and swallowed at the way Aiden's eyes widened. "Edward and his boyfriend were at the party."

"Shit." Aiden stepped closer. "Were they the two guys I saw you talking with?" His eyes went hard as he flicked his gaze back in the direction they'd just come. "What did they say to you?"

"Nothing. I mean ... Never mind, it doesn't matter." Except that was a lie. Edward's and Stanton's words *did* matter. Especially Stanton's. They'd helped Zac understand that he'd wanted (dreamed of) impossible things and that he needed to get his head back on straight before he ended up hurt. "We talked, and it wasn't great, but I'm fine."

"I'm not sure you are."

Aiden raised a hand to Zac's cheek, and for just a second, Zac leaned into his touch. Craved it more than ever because Aiden always made Zac feel so good. Centered and whole, even when Zac's world was on shaky ground, and like Aiden could give Zac everything he needed without even trying.

You'll drag him down just like you did Edward.

"Goodnight, Aiden."

Zac made himself step backward even as Aiden reached for him.

"Hey, no—don't walk away now. Let me come up for a minute, and we can talk some more."

"That's not a good idea." Zac crossed his arms over his chest. "I need you to give me some space."

"I … okay? But I don't want to leave it like this. Can I call you tomorrow?"

"I'd rather you didn't."

Aiden simply stared at Zac for a long moment, and then looked so gutted Zac almost lost his nerve.

"Oh, Zac. Don't do this." Aiden's voice came out strained. "I don't know what happened back there with your ex or if I said the wrong thing, but please, please, don't do this."

"I have to, Aiden. I've been telling myself that this thing between us could work, but I should have known better."

"Don't say that."

"It's true." Zac's throat ached. "We're not a good match. I think you know it deep down because I certainly do. We don't make sense together."

"You're wrong. You have to be!" Aiden exclaimed. "For the first time in my life, everything I'm feeling makes sense, and that's because of you!"

The distress so clear in Aiden's eyes made Zac's heart ache as he forced out more words. "You won't feel like this forever."

Aiden recoiled like he'd been struck. "I disagree," he said, his voice rough.

"That's because you're young. So young, Aiden, with so much life ahead of you."

Aiden threw his arms wide. "A life I would be happy to share with you! But you won't let me in. And … I don't understand why." He dropped his arms, everything about him drooping as if he'd run out of steam. "Why won't you let me?"

"Because I can't." Zac's voice shook. "I'm not like you. I can't just open myself up to people because it hurts too much when things don't work out."

"So that's it? You're just assuming things will go bad between

72

us without even giving it a chance?"

"You forget. I've been here before. With Edward."

Aiden flinched again. "I am *not* your ex, Zac. Tell me you know that!"

"Of course, I do. But you *are* like him in so many ways. In more ways than I feel comfortable with." Zac breathed in deeply when Aiden's hands fisted. "I'm sorry I have to say that, but after what I've been through over the last two years, I know what I need. I need to end this, even though you'll think me cruel, but please know I'm doing this for *both* of us."

"You're not doing this for me!"

"I *am*. You're not going to want me in a few years and then—"

"You have no idea what I want!"

"Probably not. But I know what I want. And I don't want this, Aiden. Us. I don't want it anymore."

Aiden's throat worked in a convulsive swallow. Zac braced himself for more arguing, but everything in him lurched when Aiden turned away instead, his shoulders tight with tension. They were both silent for several beats, then Aiden raised a hand. He scrubbed at his face, motions rough, but his eyes were red and shining with tears when he finally turned around.

Oh, Aiden.

Zac uncrossed his arms, sure his heart stopped beating.

"I want to be there for you," Aiden said, his voice very, very quiet. "Be what you need. Make you happy. Make you feel the way I do when we're together. I thought that's what you ... Fuck."

He stepped forward slowly, as if unsure Zac would let him get near. "I'm sorry I couldn't do those things for you." Movements tentative, Aiden reached out and grasped two of Zac's fingers with his own, then quickly dropped them again. "I really hope you find him someday, Zac. You deserve to be happy."

Jamming his hands in his pockets, Aiden walked away, his shoulders hunched and his long legs carrying him away into the night. Zac watched him disappear and stood unmoving for some time afterward. He felt cold and empty long after he'd gone upstairs to his apartment, and his fingers ached where Aiden had held them.

Chapter Eight

Zac didn't feel any less cold or empty in the days that followed, particularly as the city around him seemed to come even more alive as Hanukkah and Christmas drew ever closer. The colored lights grew brighter and the winter air crisper, and everywhere Zac went, he heard Christmas carols and people wishing each other well. Even the food trucks outside of the hospital had been decorated with colored bulbs and bows. Not that Zac could bring himself to go anywhere near the trucks. Hell, he was having enough trouble finding an appetite for any kind of food, which was why he was sitting at the kitchen island in his apartment and not eating a salad when his mother called. At least, the sight of her aggressively ugly holiday sweater made him want to smile.

"Hola, Mama."

"Hola, querido. Que me quentas?"

"Dinner." He paused. "Maybe TV afterward. That's, uh, quite a sweater you have going on there."

"I know it's hideous, but I love it anyway." She heaved a mighty sigh. "I hate that you don't even attempt to lie about not using Spanish. But you also look a bit tired, so I'll cut you some slack. Did you work last night?"

"Mmmhmm. Where's Papa?"

"Running an errand. He's been wrapping presents since this

morning and somehow used up all the tape." Marta smirked. "What are you doing next week for Christmas?"

"Not sure." Zac made his shoulders move up and down. "Probably more of this with some extra sleeping involved."

Something in his tone caught Marta's ear. "Are you all right?"

"Sure." He cut his gaze toward the windows, then refocused on the screen. "Actually, no."

His mother sat forward in her seat. "What's wrong?"

"I was seeing someone, Mama." Zac ran a hand over his beard. "Someone wonderful. He was kind to me. Cooked for me. Liked me even though …"

"Even though what?"

"Even though I'm old and boring, and I look like this. I still don't know why either. But Aiden didn't seem to mind." Zac's chuckle hurt his throat.

"Is that how you see yourself?" The pain in his mother's tone snagged Zac's attention. "Because the rest of the world does not. I certainly don't."

"No? I thought …" Zac quickly shook his head. "Never mind."

"Wait." Marta stared at him through the phone's little screen. "Don't you tell me to never mind. Tell me what's been going on instead. Why you would think that *I* see you like that."

"Mama—"

"*Zacarías.*" Marta's accent had grown sharper, a sign that she was truly upset. "I don't want to have to get on a plane to have this conversation, but I will if I have to."

Zac sighed. "Okay, okay."

"What is going on in your head right now?" Marta asked again, her tone gentler. "You said you're old and boring, and that you look—"

"Like a man who used to be fat and maybe still is." Zac watched his mother's eyes go wide and scrubbed his forehead with one hand.

"You are *not* fat, querido." She made a helpless motion at the screen with one hand. "You look perfect to me!"

"Right now maybe," Zac said. "Because I watch what I eat, and I exercise most days—"

"Things that are good for you," Marta argued.

"Of course, yes. But what if I stopped?"

"If I gained five, ten, twenty pounds, would you find me less attractive? Like me less?"

Aiden's words echoed loudly through Zac's head. Staring hard at his mother, his throat ached even more. "What if I stopped the diet and exercise, Mama, and gained weight? Would you ... would that change the way you feel about me?"

Make you love me less?

The unspoken question burned in his lungs as Marta's eyes grew bright with tears.

"Never," she said. "You being bigger or smaller has nothing to do with the way I feel about you."

Zac drew a shaky breath. "I think I've wondered about that for years."

"But why?" Sorrow made Marta's voice thin. "How can you ask me such a thing?"

Regret worked its way through Zac at the devastation he read on his mother's face.

"I'm sorry. I didn't mean to upset you. It's just that my weight has always been so important to you."

"Your *health* has always been important to me," Marta fired back. "I made sure you ate well because I was afraid of what could happen otherwise, Zac, and I love you too much to just sit back and do nothing."

"But that's not how it feels when you come at me about my weight, Mama," Zac said. "When you tell me to be careful around friends who like to cook because they'll undo all the hard work I've put into staying this size." He ran a hand over his beard. "I *know* in my brain that you do it because you care. But it doesn't feel like caring or love. It just makes me feel bad. And then I have to wonder what would happen if I failed?"

"Oh, Zac." The tears in Marta's eyes spilled over. "You could never fail me. Never! I am so proud of you and the things you have accomplished, and of the man you've become."

For a moment, Zac didn't trust himself to speak. "Thank you," he said at last, his emotions a jumbled mess of both relief and sorrow. "I needed to hear that more than I ever realized."

"Then I will say it as many times as you need to believe it. I'm sorry if you've ever doubted that. If anything I said made you doubt me or yourself." Marta wiped her eyes. "Talk to me, hijo. Tell me why you're sad. And tell me about this Aiden you were seeing. Maybe more talking will help you feel better. And me too."

Talking to his mom *had* felt good. Zac also thought it prepared him for the moment Gianna and Mark found him in the nurses' lounge later that week because he wasn't particularly surprised when he glanced up from his book and found them standing by his table.

"Mind if we sit?" Gianna asked.

"Of course not." Zac straightened in his seat and pushed away his uneaten salad. He tried to summon a smile as they sat and started unpacking a black cloth bag, but that smile died when Gianna slid a familiar brown takeout box his way.

"Thank you, but I'm not very hungry, Gianna," he said.

"Indulge me." Her voice was gentle, and she watched Zac for a beat before she popped the lid of her own box.

Mark set a hand over one of Zac's. "You okay?"

"Yeah." Zac heaved a big sigh. "I'm so sorry if this is making things awkward for you," he said to Gianna.

"It's not great," Gianna replied, "but thanks for saying that. And you don't need to worry about avoiding the truck on my account, or Aiden's. He'll be at the Test Kitchen across town from now on. Although ... well, Emmett's still working out on the truck, and odds are good he'll want to bitch you out. So just keep that in mind."

Any hope Zac had of his appetite coming back disappeared completely. "Why did Aiden move over to the Test Kitchen?"

"He doesn't want you to be uncomfortable. It's easier for him, too."

Zac slid his hand out from under Mark's so he could pull off his glasses and bury his face in his palms. "Shit. I really fucked this up."

Gianna laid a hand on his shoulder and squeezed. "Yeah."

"I didn't mean to hurt him."

"I know."

Zac dropped his hands and stared at his friends. "I didn't know how to let him go without it being so fucking painful."

"I'm not sure why you let him go at all." Mark shook his head, a crease working its way between his brows. "What happened, Zac? Because however hard it's been on Aiden since you called things off, it's very clear to me that you're not happy about having done it."

"I'm not," Zac said. "I got scared, I guess. Everything happened so fast with Aiden, you know? We've hardly known each other more than a month, and it's like one day we were friends hanging out, and the next we were dating, and I just wasn't ready for any of it."

"I think that's crap." Mark forked up some pasta. "You can argue all you want, buddy, but the guy I've watched float around here since before Friendsgiving was happy, unlike the miserable S.O.B. sitting in front of me now."

"I know." Zac scrubbed a hand over his head. "And yes, fine, I was happy of course. Aiden's ... wonderful. But that doesn't mean we're right for each other."

Mark frowned. "How do you know you're not?"

"I have the same question," Gianna said, and Zac could hear the hesitation in her next words. "Aiden said you're worried about him being younger than you."

"I am. He's *much* younger than I am, Gianna."

"Not much younger than Owen is compared to me," Mark put in. "We've got eleven years between us—"

"And Aiden and I have fifteen," Zac began before Mark cut him off again.

"And, what—four extra years makes it impossible to have a relationship?"

"No, but I'm not you, Mark. I can't just make a thing happen because I will it to."

"Okay, boomer."

"I swear to God, I hate you so much."

"Boys." Gianna pinned them both with what looked like a glare, but Zac could tell she was trying not to laugh too. "What I started to say, Zac, is that I understand your concern. Particularly after the way things played out with your ex, who was also younger than you. Yes, Aiden told me some of what happened with you and Edward," she added, though Zac hadn't asked, and sympathy shone in her dark eyes. "But you need to remember that Aiden's not like your ex."

Zac sighed. "I know. I swear I do, Gianna, but I don't think it will matter in the long run."

"Because you're convinced he'll lose interest in you and leave?" She pressed her lips into a thin line when Zac gave her a jerky nod. "Well, then I can say categorically that you're not being fair to Aiden. He's different from a lot of people his age. He's had to be." A shadow crossed Gianna's features.

"He isn't careless with his emotions or his heart, and he'd never hurt you the way your ex did, Zac. I'm not even sure Aiden has it in him to do that to someone he cares about."

To his horror, Zac's eyes stung. "You don't know how badly I wish I could believe you."

"You can. You just have to trust him."

"Trusting Aiden's not what I worry about. I know I put it all on him and said I didn't trust he'd stay, but it's about trusting *myself* too. I don't trust my instincts or my head anymore and definitely not my heart."

"Jesus, Zac." The sorrow in Mark's voice made Zac bite the inside of his cheek.

Gianna almost smiled though. "Aiden can teach you how to trust yourself again. He has a genius for affection. You just have to let him in."

Zac could only nod. His friend sounded so confident. A hundred times more sure than Zac that she was right about ... well, everything. He really had fucked things up. Hurt himself. Hurt Aiden too, which was so much worse because Aiden hadn't done anything wrong. He deserved better treatment. And he definitely deserved an apology, provided he would even speak to Zac.

Knowing all that made Zac's trip across town later that afternoon both easier and harder. His nerves increased as he approached Federal Street, but he paused after catching sight of the store and its big glass windows. The Test Kitchen was brightly lit, which made it easy to see everyone in the store, even from outside. Zac spied Aiden immediately, but rather than cooking he was seated at a long table in what appeared to be a glass room that bisected the Test Kitchen through its center and split one large space into two. Unlike the last time Zac'd seen him, Aiden wore his usual t-shirt and bandana, and he was making notes on a tablet that held his attention despite the activity surrounding him. He didn't glance up as Zac entered the store.

"I'm a friend of Aiden's," Zac said to the young woman who greeted him from behind the counter. "He's not expecting me though, so is it all right if I—"

"You can just go on in." She gestured toward the door. "Aiden won't mind. He's got an open-door policy unless he's on the phone, and honestly, a lot of people knock on the windows just to wave and say hi. He always waves back."

Zac smiled. Yes, that sounded very much like Aiden. "Thank you."

As he got closer, he noticed a sign on the glass that read "Aiden's Office" and smiled again, but he had to steel himself before he could push open the door. The way the curiosity on Aiden's face melted into blankness after he'd glanced up made Zac glad he hadn't simply tapped on the glass.

The poor kid looks like he saw a ghost.

"Hi, Aiden. Can I come in?"

Aiden seemed to shake himself. "Of course." He set the tablet down and waved Zac in, blinking rapidly as he straightened in his seat. "Sorry. You, um, caught me by surprise."

That hesitation snagged Zac's conscience as he sat down across the table from Aiden, as did Aiden's weary appearance. He looked gorgeous of course, but careworn too, with dark shadows under his eyes and more stubble on his face than Zac had ever seen. Even so, Aiden's expression was kind as he met Zac's gaze.

"What are you doing in this part of town, Zac? You get lost on your way to lunch?"

"Maybe a little. I had to see you."

Aiden's brow furrowed. "Do you need something?"

Zac swallowed hard. Despite the thudding of his heart against his ribs, he knew he'd been right to come. Whatever Aiden thought of him—however much pain he'd been in since Zac had shut him out—he wasn't turning Zac away. That wasn't particularly surprising given what Zac already knew about Aiden. He was kinder than Zac deserved and had a wide-open heart he was willing to share, even with someone who'd hurt him.

"Yes, I need something," Zac said. He pulled off his glasses. "I need you to disregard the things I said to you the other night. And I need to apologize. Because I was terribly unfair to you, and I feel awful about that. I'm sorry, Aiden. Truly."

A flush worked its way over Aiden's cheeks. Sitting back in his chair, he dropped his gaze and crossed his arms over his chest. "Thank you for saying that." His voice had gone gruff, and he moved the fingers of his left hand over the tattoo sleeve on his skin. "It means ... It means a lot that you did."

An ache filtered through Zac at the tightness in Aiden's tone. "If you can forgive me, I'd like to try again. Start over from scratch."

"I'd ... like that," Aiden said, his voice still low. "Very much. I'm just not sure—" He stayed quiet a moment, and there was fear in his eyes when he raised them to meet Zac's. "I don't want to mess up again and hurt us both."

Oh, baby.

God, he looked so sad. Zac held a hand out over the table, his heart pounding even harder when Aiden immediately reached out and took it. "You didn't do anything wrong. You didn't mess up either. I did. And I'm working to make sure I don't do it again. Or at least, not in such spectacular fashion. Outside of working with patients, I am incapable of getting anything right the first time."

That cracked Aiden's frown. "Lucky for your patients, huh?" He chuckled then, and the sound made Zac do the same. They sat silently for a time, hands joined over the table while the hesitation in Aiden's face slowly faded along with the ache in Zac's chest. Finally, Aiden cracked a small smile.

"So, what do we do now?"

Zac hauled in what felt like his first deep breath in days. "Well, I have to go back to the hospital—I'm working a double. But I'm off for a couple days starting tomorrow morning, and I wondered if I could make you dinner. We can talk some more? Once I'm, you know, awake again."

"You're cooking?"

"I'd like to. At my apartment actually. If you trust me not to burn pancakes anyway."

Aiden's eyes lit up. "Pancakes, huh?"

"They're the only thing I know how to cook that doesn't involve a microwave." Zac sniffed at Aiden's laughter but reveled in the warmth rolling through him. "I'll need help with the bacon."

"The fact you're even *open* to eating bacon with me sounds perfect," Aiden said. "What time do you want me there?"

"Is six too early? I wasn't kidding when I said I might need help, so if you want to eat before midnight—"

"Six is fine. I put myself on the early shift for tomorrow, so there should be no problem if I run out before close."

"Great." Zac glanced at his watch, then worried his bottom lip with his teeth. "I've got to get back across town, but you'll call if you change your mind?"

"Yes. I won't change my mind though." Aiden nodded at the

windows. "Not sure those bozos out there would let me either."

Puzzled, Zac glanced over his shoulder and saw that many of the customers and staff beyond the glass were watching him and Aiden, and all of them were smiling. He swallowed a laugh as heat licked at his cheeks.

"Oops. Didn't mean to make a scene."

"Eh, it's okay. Serves me right for agreeing to a literal glass office." Aiden gave Zac his biggest smile so far. "But I'll walk you out and make sure no one gives you a hard time."

Chapter Nine

Just after six the next evening, the concierge in Zac's building rang his phone. Zac knew why of course, but that didn't stop him from staring at the number on the screen like he'd never seen it before.

As much as he'd looked forward to this dinner, Zac's nerves were unsettled. He'd wanted to invite Aiden into his home yesterday—the relief that had gone through him after he'd done it had been intense. Even now, he smiled at the memory of the way Aiden's eyes had shone as he'd escorted Zac out onto the sidewalk outside of the Endless Pastabilities Test Kitchen. However, it had been a long time since Zac had let someone so far into his life, and for all his conviction, he was off balance. The walls he'd constructed around himself after Edward had left were shaky but still very much standing, and he knew it would take time to fully rid himself of the ghosts of his failed relationship. Whether Aiden would be willing to stick around long enough for that to happen, Zac didn't know.

Come on, man. Give the kid a chance.

That the voice in his head suddenly sounded like Mark made Zac laugh hard, and it was a moment before he could collect himself enough to take the call and ask the concierge to send Aiden on up.

He went to the door at Aiden's knock and opened it to find him holding a holiday wreath fashioned from fresh holly, one of his many black cloth bags over his shoulder. Aiden's eyes were glowing under the brim of a wool tweed cap Zac had never seen before, and he'd shaved. Zac could tell he'd showered after finishing work too from the woody smell of his shower gel.

"Come in," Zac said and took Aiden's arm as he stepped over the threshold. "Is this wreath for me?"

"If you want it," Aiden said with a shy smile. "I remember you saying you never have time to decorate, so I figured I'd help. I have a couple strings of lights too."

Without thinking, Zac drew Aiden into a hug and closed his eyes as Aiden pressed a soft kiss to his cheek.

There.

"I brought some blackberries and crème fraiche from the market near my place," Aiden said then. He pulled away, licking his lips as he handed the bag to Zac. "And there's a bottle of Vouvray in there too. I've always found it goes well with crepes, so I thought that maybe it would be okay with pancakes. Or we could make coffee instead, or whatever—"

"Aiden, stop."

Zac fished the bottle out of the bag. Aiden's nervous rambling was adorable but sobering too. Clearly, Zac wasn't the only person feeling adrift tonight. Damned if that didn't make him feel even more guilty about what he'd put them through.

"Thank you for the wreath and the wine and … thank you," he said with a smile he hoped would put Aiden at ease. "I've never had wine and pancakes before. You realize they're just begging to be burned now."

"Hey, I'm a professional." Aiden followed Zac deeper into the apartment, which was set up in an open plan with a wall of windows in front of them. "Consider me back up for all your kitchen needs. I can help you hang up the wreath and lights too, if you'd like."

"I'll take you up on that," Zac said. "But let me open this first and show you around the place. Not that you can't see basically everything for yourself from here. Can I get you a glass now?"

"Sure, thanks. Coat goes in the closet?"

Zac barely managed not to roll his eyes at himself. "Sorry, yes. Worst host ever."

"You're fine. This is a great place. Oh, hey, you've got a balcony!"

"It's one of my favorite features of the apartment," Zac said. "There's a pool on the roof too, which is nice, but I prefer your view. It's more dramatic."

"That's why it suits me. Oh, this has got to be Gordon."

"The one and only." Throwing a glance over his shoulder at the orange cat who'd roused itself at the sound of a new voice, Zac stepped into the kitchen area and busied himself opening the bottle. He didn't turn around again until he'd filled two glasses, and he froze at the sight of Aiden, dressed in a casual sweater and jeans, the cat in his arms and tweed cap nowhere in sight, his brown hair shaved down to a mere inch of fuzz on top and even shorter on the sides and back.

"Holy shit." Zac's voice was hushed.

Without his soft curls, Aiden's cheekbones and strong jawline were even more sharply defined, and his eyes appeared larger. Bending forward, he set Gordon on the floor.

"You cut your hair," Zac said stupidly.

"Yeah." Aiden's mouth lifted up on one side. "You didn't notice yesterday because I was wearing the bandana." He crossed his arms again, and Zac knew that if he'd been wearing short sleeves instead of the cable-knit sweater, Aiden would be running his fingers over the tattooed swirls on his skin. He looked very young and achingly uncertain. "Emmett and I got drunk and shaved each other's heads."

Zac blinked. "Why?"

Aiden arched an eyebrow. "Doesn't the drunk part go a ways toward explaining why?"

"I—not exactly." Zac shook his head. "Why shave off your hair?"

"I was talking about getting another tattoo. Apparently."

"Apparently? Don't you know?"

Aiden's ears reddened as he accepted a glass of wine from Zac. "No. We were drinking tequila, and that evening goes a bit in and out. From what Emmett said, he wasn't about to let me near a tattoo studio, so he somehow talked me into cutting off my hair instead. I'm not sure why the idea shut me up, but here we are."

The mental image those words conjured up made Zac bite back a wince. "And why did Emmett shave his head?"

"I dared him to." Aiden shrugged and sipped from his glass. "*That* I remember with clarity. I didn't think he'd let me, you know—still can't believe he did. But after he was finished with mine, he handed me the clippers and told me to go ahead."

"I see." Zac wasn't sure how else to respond. He'd gotten to know Emmett enough to recognize that impulsive acts like head shaving weren't entirely off brand. Aiden was a different story, however.

"Sean was pissed at us both," Aiden went on. "He's the one who had to go back to fix the spots we missed the next morning, make us look more presentable." Aiden rubbed at the fuzz again with his free hand, smiling faintly. "Made us clean up all the hair we tracked around the apartment too. Didn't have much sympathy for our epic hangovers."

"I can imagine."

"He got over it. Especially because the short hair works for Em."

Zac stepped closer, then carefully reached up and ran his hand over the fuzz on Aiden's head, smiling at the way the fine bristles tickled his fingertips.

"Oh! So soft." His smile got wider when Aiden grimaced. "You don't like it?"

"Not really." Aiden sniffed. "I look like a baby bird."

"No, you don't." Zac moved his hand and cupped Aiden's cheek. "You look great."

His smile faded at the apprehension he read in Aiden's gaze.

Then Aiden covered Zac's hand with his own, and Zac leaned in so he could brush his lips against Aiden's. His insides flipped when Aiden's other arm came around Zac's waist. Aiden's eyelids fluttered and closed, and desire rippled through Zac as he closed his eyes too and kissed Aiden deeper.

Oh, yes, Zac had missed this. Missed connecting with Aiden through touch and taste, the press of their bodies together, and the way his fingers tingled as he dropped their joined hands from Aiden's jaw. He moved to pull Aiden into his arms and remembered the glass in his hand only after wine sloshed over his knuckles and splashed onto the floor.

"Oops."

Aiden's gentle laugh ghosted sweet over Zac's lips. "We should make dinner before we wreck your kitchen," he said and pressed another fast kiss against Zac's mouth. "I don't have a change of clothes either, so keep your wine in your glass."

Zac wanted to get close to Aiden far more than he wanted food, but instinct told him to follow Aiden's lead. If he needed to take things slow right now, Zac could get on board. God knew Aiden had been patient when Zac had needed a slower pace. Aiden also hadn't steered Zac wrong yet, and Zac certainly couldn't say the same.

They fell into a more natural rhythm as they worked on the meal, and though Zac should have felt some nerves about cooking beside a trained chef, he reminded himself that this chef was Aiden, and he'd never judge Zac if the pancakes turned out dry. Which, to Zac's immense satisfaction, didn't happen because he turned out three stacks of the most perfect pancakes he'd ever flipped.

As promised, Aiden fried the bacon, sneaking the occasional blackberry as he worked and hummed along to Zac's Beatles playlist. But soon, his impish nature seemed to take hold. Before Zac could protest, Aiden had seized two of the stacks and deftly layered strips of bacon between the cakes, then buttered each and drizzled everything with just the right amount of syrup.

"Goddamn it, Aiden. I can feel my arteries hardening just

looking at these … things."

Aiden smiled at his own handiwork. "Is that your way of saying you won't eat them?"

"I said no such thing."

"Yeah? Because I left the third stack alone, just in case you didn't want one of these monsters."

"You're sweet to do that, but I'm in the mood for a little monster eating." Zac picked the platter up from the counter. He meant every word. This was the first time he'd been truly hungry since the argument with Aiden. "Now come on before I just put my face into one of these."

"Oh, I see how it is." Aiden's tone was dry. "You'll eat my monster stacks of pancakes but won't even show me around your apartment."

"Crap." Zac carried the platter to the kitchen island that he preferred over his minuscule dining table and set it down. "I blame you," he said as they both rounded the island and slid onto seats. "You scrambled my brain with the haircut. And the kissing."

"Hey, you kissed me, man."

"That I did."

"Feel free to do it again."

So Zac leaned in and kissed Aiden again, savoring the tastes of salt and wine and berries on his lips.

"I'll show you around as soon as we finish eating," he said after they'd surfaced again. Without thinking, he reached up to push the hair back from Aiden's forehead, then pulled back when his fingers met fuzz. "Huh."

"Damn it," Aiden muttered. His ears went red as he turned to his food. "I could kill Emmett for digging out those clippers."

A stiff silence fell over the table, and Zac frowned at Aiden's downcast eyes.

"Aiden, you didn't answer my question earlier when I asked why you shaved your head. That doesn't sound like something you'd do."

"Yeah, well. Haven't really felt like myself lately."

"Because of what happened at the holiday party?"

Aiden's eyes were guarded when he looked up. "No. I don't know what happened at the party, Zac. Only that when I came back from meeting people, you were checked out. And when I tried to talk to you about it, you told me we were wrong for each other and you didn't want me anymore."

Fuck.

Zac drew a breath to see if he still could. "I'm sorry. I didn't mean any of it."

"Yeah, you said that. I can tell you think you mean it too."

"I do."

"But I still don't know what the fuck happened, other than you ran into your ex."

"And I know that doesn't excuse any of it either." Zac sighed. "Seeing Edward and his boyfriend, Stanton, at the party rattled me. I didn't know they'd be there, and I wasn't … *ready* to see them. They wanted to talk about you, of course. They were only there because Stanton wanted to meet you."

"Oh, hell." Aiden laid his hand over Zac's at once. That comforting, familiar weight and the empathy in his eyes was almost too much to bear. "I'm sorry. If I'd known who they were—"

"No." Zac flipped his hand up and slid his fingers around Aiden's. "You have nothing to be sorry for. And neither does Stanton for wanting to meet you. I just wish I'd handled it better."

"Handled what better?"

"All of it. Stanton and his bullshit in particular. But I let him get in my head, just like he used to back when he was the shittiest friend I could have asked for."

"Oh, man." Aiden grimaced. "You sure can pick 'em."

Zac huffed out a laugh, then picked up his fork with his free hand. "Yeah, I know. But Stanton's not the only asshole. Yes, he acts like a shit, but Edward stands by and does nothing while I take it. Each of us is as dysfunctional as the next."

His forehead puckered, Aiden gave Zac's fingers another squeeze, then turned him loose. "Don't you think you're being a little hard on yourself?"

"No." Zac took a bite and chewed for a moment before he spoke again. "Damn, those are good. But, Aiden, it's been almost two years since Edward left. I've been trying to get my head back on straight since then, and I thought I was gaining some ground by the time you and I met. But all it took were a few words from Stanton for him to cut me down, and I shouldn't *let* him or Edward affect me that way. They have no right to do so, and if I hadn't let them, I wouldn't have said those things to you. Wouldn't even have thought the words to begin with."

"Why did you say them?" Aiden asked, his voice quieter.

"I was scared. Still am."

"Of what?"

Zac set his fork down and reached for his wine. "Of you, if I'm honest. Or rather myself with you. You're a lot younger than I am, and we're at very different places in our lives. You already know my work schedule can make it hard to have a social life. Sometimes, I'm just too tired. I enjoy the things you and I have been doing together, but at the same time, I can't help wonder if it's enough for you."

Aiden slipped some food in his mouth and chewed in silence before he answered. "Zac, if I wanted to do different things with you or even without you, I'd say so."

Zac set a hand on Aiden's forearm. "I know."

"I'm also going to call bullshit if you say you haven't noticed that my schedule is unforgiving too." He met Zac's gaze. "I work weekends. My days are long, even when I'm finished cooking. I'm up at five more mornings than I'm not, and it is not a lie when I say I'm fucking wiped by ten at night."

"I know all that. But Edward and I used to argue about my schedule interfering with our social lives, and I guess it's become habit for me to worry about it even now."

After a long pause, Aiden gave Zac a smile. He nodded at Zac's plate, so Zac dug in again, savoring the sweet and salty flavors as Aiden told him about changes he planned for the Endless

Pastabilities menu. Even so, Zac had come to know Aiden well enough to understand something was off. A line had carved its way between Aiden's eyebrows, and he was pushing food around his plate more than truly eating it. And the longer it went on, the more Zac's stomach sank at the realization that whatever was bothering Aiden, he didn't seem ready to share it with Zac.

Finally, Zac set everything down and reached up to brush his hand against the side of Aiden's neck, his heart throbbing when Aiden quickly ducked his head and dropped a tender kiss against Zac's knuckles.

"Are you all right?" He frowned when Aiden's eyes fell closed.

"Sure."

"Aiden. What is it?"

Aiden drew a long breath in through his nose, but rather than answering, he opened his eyes and reached for the plates.

"I'll just get the fruit—"

"No, come on." Moving quickly, Zac placed his hands on Aiden's wrists to keep him still. "What aren't you saying to me?"

Aiden's face was somber. "Don't you trust me at all, Zac?"

"Yes, I do." Zac wanted to sigh at the doubt he saw so clearly in Aiden's eyes. "I know I've said this before, but I'm the problem, not you. I misjudged Edward and Stanton so badly and knowing that makes it hard for me to judge what is best and what will work in my own life."

"And again, I call bullshit." Aiden's gaze heated, though his voice remained measured. "I know we haven't been seeing each other for very long, but I'm part of this too. You can't take all of the blame onto yourself, which means some of it *is* on me. And if you feel you can't trust yourself around me then I must be doing something wrong."

"But you're not. You've been perfect, actually. For me and to me, as well." Zac shook his head when Aiden sighed. "I told you before that I'm finding it hard to let people in. I've been working on that, but it takes time, and I'm going to make mistakes." He swallowed, rubbing Aiden's wrists with his fingers as he struggled to find his words. "That said, I've been feeling more like myself for the first time in a very long while. I feel good, and a lot of that is because of you."

Aiden flipped his hands to catch hold of Zac's, and he pulled him in for a kiss that was slow and sweet and perfect.

"I'm not Edward," he said when they'd come back up again. "And I'm not planning on going anywhere."

"Okay," Zac said at once. He believed Aiden's earnest words and, even more, wanted badly to erase the hurt on Aiden's handsome face. "I don't want to be anywhere else either."

"Good." Aiden set his forehead on Zac's shoulder and blew out a long breath. "I'd like to get used to having you around again then."

Zac rubbed Aiden's back. "That sounds like a plan I can get behind."

After dinner, Aiden helped Zac hang the wreath on the door and string white fairy lights in a zigzag pattern across the big windows while Gordon the cat stared at them, his green eyes aglow. Zac also made good on his promise to show Aiden around the apartment, and a genuine, deep pleasure ran through him when, after the quick tour, Aiden settled on the long couch with Gordon by his side.

"Again, nice place," Aiden said. "Very neat and tidy, and no fuss. Suits you."

"You just called me boring, didn't you?" Zac chuckled when Aiden rolled his eyes. "I like it too. Like the neighborhood and that the building is close to the hospital. And I *love* this couch." He settled down beside Aiden. "Being able to come home after a long shift and veg out in comfort is one of my favorite things to do."

"You sleep out here?"

"More than I'd like to admit. The couch was one of the first things I bought after moving in here," Zac said. "Of course, I'd unloaded almost all of the stuff Edward left behind, so I mean it when I say I needed somewhere to sit."

"Why'd you dump everything?"

"I wanted to start over, I guess." Zac shrugged. "Seemed …
like the right thing to do after things had gone so wrong. I sold and
donated what I could, and my sister and a couple of friends helped
me make this place livable. I'm so glad to be back in the city again
too."

Aiden eyed him curiously. "Yeah? You don't miss the suburbs
at all?"

"No. We only moved to Arlington because Edward wanted the
house and yard. He liked being able to show off all our hard work.
Once we were out there though, he realized our friends weren't
going to follow us. That's when he started complaining about living
too far from all the interesting places to go out."

"I've been to Arlington." Aiden sipped his wine. "The center of
town is pretty nice. Not to mention being, like, literal minutes from
Somerville, Cambridge, *and* Boston."

"Oh, I know," Zac said. "We spent a lot of time *not* being in
Arlington when I wasn't working night shifts. And when I was,
Edward would hang out with friends. He still wanted to go out and
have a good time when I wasn't around."

Zac's smile felt tight, but the bitterness he'd held onto for so
long had lessened. Lost its power really, and knowing that made
him feel lighter, even as he talked about it. Zac found he didn't
mind talking about it now, or at least he didn't with Aiden.

"We tried to make it work, but Edward always seemed restless.
I never thought he'd look for someone else though." He frowned.
"Sure, I knew things weren't perfect, but it caught me by surprise
when everything blew up. And then I forced Edward into couple's
therapy, which was an unmitigated disaster, and we ended up
splitting anyway."

"Ugh." Aiden squeezed Zac's hand. "I'm sorry he hurt you."

"Me too. But it's time I put it behind me, and I'm ready to do
that." Letting go of Aiden's hand, Zac raised both of his to frame
Aiden's face and draw him close.

He sighed when Aiden kissed him deeper this time. Aiden slid
his fingers beneath the collar of Zac's shirt, and Zac moved

without thought, easing out of his seat and pushing Aiden back so Zac could settle onto his lap. Fire raced through Zac at Aiden's low groan. They wound their arms around each other, straining to get closer, and if Zac could have crawled inside Aiden, he would have. He shuddered when Aiden rocked beneath him and pulled away to catch his breath.

"Lie down with me?"

"I can't." Aiden pressed his forehead into Zac's shoulder with a ragged exhale. "Fuck me, but I need to get going."

Zac frowned and ran a hand over Aiden's fuzzy head. "Why?"

"Emmett's picking me up early tomorrow morning so we can drive up to Portland and meet with a guy who's interested in joining the team."

"I'm confused. Why isn't the Portland guy coming to you?"

"This guy wants to join the team *from* Portland." Aiden drew circles over Zac's shoulders with his hands. "He's already got a team in a truck in the city center and thinks they'd do well there selling my food."

Zac blinked in surprise as Aiden's words sunk in. "You mean you'd expand Endless Pastabilities into Portland? That's fantastic."

Aiden raised his head, a smile in his eyes. "It's an exciting prospect, yeah. Nothing's been decided yet though. Em and I are meeting the truck owner tomorrow to hear his pitch and check out Portland, but that's as far as we've gone." He pushed his lips into a pout. "Sort of wish I could cancel now, but the meeting's already set up, and we want to get it done before the holidays start this weekend."

"Don't even think about canceling," Zac scolded. He kissed Aiden gently. "And no apologies either. Of course, I want you here. I also know how important Endless Pastabilities is to you."

He shifted so he could get up, but Aiden tightened his grip on Zac. He buried his face in Zac's chest and hummed when Zac nuzzled the crown of Aiden's head with his lips.

"This is important to me too," Aiden said in a soft voice. "Right here, right now, with you."

Zac lay in bed after Aiden had gone, his lips kiss swollen, and his mind on the empty space beside him. He'd pushed Aiden against the wall as they'd waited for his Lyft, and the memory of Aiden's gasp as they ground against each other made Zac's stomach flutter and his dick stiffen.

He wrapped his fingers around himself and groaned, picturing Aiden above him, settling between Zac's legs while their cocks slid together. He imagined Aiden pushing inside him and the way their breaths would mix when their mouths met. Pleasure crashed through Zac in a wave that made his hips buck and his bones melt as he pumped himself and grunted, his mouth falling open and his hand flying until cum pulsed over his hand and belly.

I wish he were here.

Chapter Ten

Before he'd even left the apartment the next morning, Zac's phone started buzzing with messages from Aiden—some paired with photos—from his road trip to Portland with Emmett.

I am out of coffee. This is a serious problem.

Crisis averted: St. Emmett brought coffee & doughnuts. #bffs

Holy traffic, Batman!

Most of the photos were of Emmett or his and Aiden's surroundings, but a sweet buzz worked its way through Zac as he looked over a photo of Aiden, whose eyes were crinkled with laughter as he made a grab for the phone. All the messages made Zac smile, even when he didn't have time to reply. He'd missed those quirky trains of thought flashing across his screen even more than he realized.

Spying Gianna as he headed toward the nurses' lounge, he quickly slipped the phone in his pocket and straightened his face. Gianna's smirk told him he was too late though, and she held up a black cloth bag emblazoned with the Endless Pastabilities logo.

"I bought lunch," she said as soon as Zac was close. "Two orders of gnocchi in vodka sauce. You don't have to eat it if you don't want it of course, but at least, take it home for dinner."

"Thank you. And of course, I want to eat it."

Zac gestured for Gianna to enter the lounge before him. He'd planned to eat fewer calories today in answer (and penance) for the monster pancakes and wine he'd had at dinner the night before. Zac's plans to be good were going to have to wait a while longer though because his stomach was already rumbling at the thought of pillowy dumplings in peppery herbal sauce.

"How was your dinner with Aiden?"

"Really nice. I even managed not to burn anything."

Gianna chuckled as they took their seats. "I'm glad."

"Me, too. We talked a lot. Ate more pancakes than anyone has a right to." Zac set his lunch bag with its salad and yogurt contents on the chair beside him and accepted the box of pasta from Gianna. "It was good to spend time together again. I guess I'd gotten used to having Aiden in my life without even knowing it."

Gianna said nothing at first, but her expression sobered, and Zac could tell from the way she pursed her lips that she was weighing her words carefully. "Do you consider Aiden more than a friend, Zac?"

Zac frowned. "What do you mean?"

"I mean, do you think of Aiden more like a boyfriend than a buddy? In the longer term, I mean," Gianna quickly added when Zac raised his eyebrows high.

"I'm … not sure how to answer," Zac replied, his words slow as the word "boyfriend" crashed around in his head. Were he and Aiden boyfriends now? Had they been before Zac had screwed everything up?

"Aiden is more than a 'buddy' to me," Zac said, "but I'm not sure I can put a label on what we are. I never even thought to before today." He blew a breath out through his nose. "And I *can't* in this moment either because we're still getting past the crap I pulled after the holiday party."

Understanding filtered through Gianna's gaze. "That makes sense."

"Why do you ask?"

Instead of answering right away, Gianna turned her attention to her food. She speared gnocchi with her fork before she spoke again. "I'm sure you already know this, but Aiden took it hard when you broke things off with him."

Zac thought about the flickers of doubt he'd seen on Aiden's face throughout their evening.

"Haven't really felt like myself lately."

"I don't have plans to go anywhere."

"Don't you trust me at all?"

He'd sounded very unlike his usual cocksure self when he'd said those things to Zac.

Zac ran a hand over his beard. "I do know that. And you have no idea how badly I feel about hurting him. Even after we talked, he seemed ... I don't know. Spooked, I suppose. And like he didn't want to say too much."

Gianna chewed in silence for a while, then gave Zac a searching look. "Has Aiden told you about how he came to live with my parents and me?"

"He said his birth parents were killed in an auto accident when he was six and that your mother was a cousin of his mother." Zac cocked his head. "Why?"

"He was staying at a neighbor's house while his parents had dinner with friends. When Aiden woke up, the Daughertys were gone. He had no other relatives locally, so he went into state care while the authorities tried to track members of his family down. He was in the custody of California Social Services for a month before my mother was notified."

Zac swallowed hard at the thought of a homeless, orphaned Aiden, six years old and all alone. "I had no idea. Why did it take so long?"

Gianna sighed. "My mother and Aiden's grew up on opposite sides of the country. Mamma met that side of her family a few times, and even bonded with Aiden's mom. They were around the same age and wrote letters and sent Christmas cards back and forth for years. They never got together as adults though, and all I knew about Aiden was that he was a little cousin who lived in California." She uncapped her water and took a long sip.

"The name 'Angelina Marinelli' didn't exactly stand out in the Daughertys' papers—she could have been anyone Aiden's mom or dad knew through a dozen different ways. Social Services contacted my mom once they figured out who she was to Aiden, but even that was a pain in the ass." Gianna grimaced. "My parents work in art restoration, see, and we were in Florence when Aiden's parents were killed. It took us a few days to pack up and get back even after Mama and Pops knew."

Relief coursed through Zac at those words, even knowing that over twenty years had passed since the Marinellis had taken Aiden in. "Thank God, they found you at all. It must have been weird gaining a brother overnight."

"Weird, yes, but not terrible." Gianna nodded at Zac's food, and she waited until he'd started eating again. "Mamma and Pops fell in love with Aiden the minute they met him. Hell, I did too, and I was a misanthropic fifteen-year-old girl at the time."

"What was he like?" Zac asked around a mouthful of pasta.

"Shy, if you can believe it. Quiet and careful. And sad of course, though he tried to hide it. He held back a lot of himself. Mamma thought Aiden was afraid we'd change our minds and disappear on him too."

"The poor kid." Zac shook his head.

"It took time for him to trust us to keep him." Gianna reached for her water. "But once he got comfortable—once he knew we were going to be there for him no matter what—he let us in and became one of the most loving people I've ever met. My parents and I were happy just as we were, but our lives got even better when Aiden came to live with us."

A frown worked its way across Gianna's pretty face. "Losing people is difficult for Aiden even now, Zac. He doesn't like to lose touch with the people in his life. And maybe you can understand why it might unnerve him when a friendship with someone he cares about evaporates into thin air."

Zac blew out a long breath. He got it all right. He was going to have to work at winning back Aiden's trust.

"Aiden is very attached to you." Gianna's voice was kind, but there was steel in her eyes. "You hurt him when you cut him out. I suspect he'll worry that you're going to go cold on him again, and if you *don't* see this thing you two have going as something that could go long term—"

"It's not that I don't see it going somewhere," Zac hastened to say. Aiden wasn't the only one who'd gotten attached here. "I just need time to figure out where it'll go. Aiden needs time too, Gianna," he added when she opened her mouth to speak. "What we have *is* new for both of us, and we're going to have to figure out how it works. But I do want more with Aiden, even if I'm not sure yet what that means."

Don't you though? Because you've been falling hard for that kid almost from the start.

Zac swallowed hard at the truth in those words. He didn't have time to dwell on them either because the combined chimes of his and Gianna's phones ended their lunch, and all discussion about Aiden's frame of mind disappeared in their dash back onto the floor.

It was nearly four in the afternoon before either of them had time for another break. They'd started back toward the lounge when Zac's phone buzzed again, but this time with another text from Aiden, accompanied by a photo of Emmett, a spoon in his mouth and grinning at what appeared to be a cardboard cup full of soup.

Em's died and gone to clam chowder heaven. Idk how one person eats so much.

Smiling, Zac quickly tapped out a reply. *When are you headed back? Leaving in 10.*

Have dinner with me tonight?

I can do that. Prob back by 6:30. We cooking in or going out?

Zac found Gianna watching him when he glanced up again, and his cheeks heated at the amusement he read in her face.

"Is he sexting you?" she asked.

"No!" Zac barked out laugh. "God, no, and don't give him any ideas. I need a favor though, and I need it tonight."

"Sure," Gianna said with a shrug. "What did you have in mind?"

"I need to figure out how to cook something good that isn't pancakes in the next'"—Zac checked his watch—"two hours.'"

OoOoO

Fatigue from his trip showed in Aiden's eyes when Zac let him in later that evening, but his face lit up with a smile.

"Hey, Zac. The wreath makes the whole hallway smell nice."

"It does! And hey, yourself." Zac drew Aiden into a hug but was careful to avoid crushing the paper bag in his hand as they exchanged a quick kiss. "What have you got there?"

"Blueberry scones with rosemary," Aiden said with a leer. He handed over the bag. "We found the best vegan bakery just before we got in the car for the trip home, and Em bought his weight in cookies. These had just come out of the oven, and I thought you might like half for breakfast. They're a lot lighter than a traditional scone and—" He paused as Zac held up a hand.

"Thank you," Zac said and gave Aiden another squeeze.

After Aiden had removed his coat and cap, they moved to the kitchen where Aiden sipped a beer and chatted with Zac while he arranged their meal.

"Should I be sad we're not having pancakes again?" Aiden asked.

"I don't think so, no." Zac flashed him a smile. "While pancakes are the only thing I can cook with any kind of skill, I am well versed in the art of arranging salad. Especially if there's a pre-roasted chicken around. Tell me about your trip and how things went with the Portland food truck guy."

"It was a good day!" Aiden exclaimed. He started rolling up one sleeve of his flannel button-down shirt. "Portland's great, you know, with a fantastic food scene. We stopped a bunch of times to try things."

"Yep, I got that from your photos—I'm not sure how *either* you or Em can put away so much food and still stay so trim." Zac arranged the chicken he'd carved on a bed of romaine and red cabbage and tossed it all with sliced persimmons and pears, red onion, pomegranate seeds, and toasted pignoli. "What did you think of the food truck guy?"

"He was cool and very good at what he does." Aiden beamed at the salad bowl as Zac set it down. "Mmm, this looks yummy. Anyway, after the meeting, Em and I walked around the city all afternoon, getting a feel for the place. I can picture an Endless Pastabilities truck doing well there."

"But?" Zac prompted as he rounded the island, his eyes on Aiden's thoughtful expression.

"But, it just didn't feel right." Aiden ran his fingers over the tattoos peeking out from beneath his rolled-up sleeve. "Maybe it will someday, but now is not the time."

"You appear to be okay with the decision."

"I am." Aiden smiled when he caught Zac's searching look. "And so is Em. We agree it's an exciting idea, but we have a good thing going on with the trucks and the windows and the Kitchen here in this city. I don't want to jeopardize anything by stretching too far, too fast. Things in this business are risky enough as it is."

That was more than enough for Zac. "Good," he said, then turned to the salad bowl so he could scoop portions onto their plates.

They continued talking as they ate, but soon, Aiden had paused, and the way he stared at the food on his plate made Zac bite back a smile.

"My sister coached you," Aiden stated rather than asked, then raised his fork to his mouth and tasted the dressing that lingered there with care. "This salad dressing is one of Gia's."

"Maybe?"

"No, definitely. She's made this for me before. Walnut oil, red wine vinegar, and honey, right? The fancy organic honey from the Whole Foods Market near the hospital?"

Zac laughed loudly, enjoying the impish glee on Aiden's face far too much. "Jesus Christ, Aiden. You're a little scary right now."

"Please, this is nothing. You haven't seen scary until you've had a meal at the Test Kitchen after it closes and the team goes nuts with the molecular gastronomy techniques. Those are some freaky skills."

"What, you're worried I couldn't handle it?"

"Oh, I'm sure you could." Aiden knocked Zac's shoulder gently with his own. "A few of us are throwing down some new stuff next week on the day after Christmas, as it happens. Would you like to come?"

Aiden's voice was light, but his cheeks flushed pink, a sure sign in Zac's mind that extending this invitation was a bigger deal than he'd made it out to be. Setting a hand on Aiden's forearm, he waited until Aiden met his gaze before he answered.

"I'd like that."

They moved to Zac's sofa after dinner with a plate of fruit and cheeses, and though Zac called up a Netflix series to stream, his and Aiden's attentions were more on each other. Soon they were exchanging kisses made sweet and tart by their dessert, Aiden's eagerness obvious and his touch more confident as he moved his hands over Zac's shoulders and back. He'd started climbing onto Zac's lap when a distinctive ringtone filled the air.

"Shit, I'm sorry." Zac kissed Aiden quickly, then sat forward and reached for his phone on the table. "That's my dad."

Aiden sank back into his seat with a brilliant grin. "Your dad's ringtone is *Devil in Disguise*?"

Zac snorted as he got to his feet. "The old man likes Elvis. I'll grab this in the bedroom, but it shouldn't take long."

Jaimie Alvarez was in a talkative mood however, which didn't come as a surprise considering he'd been busy planning a dinner to celebrate his forty-fifth wedding anniversary to Zac's mother. There were a million details Zac's dad wanted to discuss, particularly now that he knew Zac had been dating a chef, and Zac was forced to promise he'd run the anniversary dinner menu by

Aiden before he could end the video chat.

Zac glanced at his watch as he made his way out of the bedroom and grimaced when he realized he'd left Aiden alone for forty minutes. Aiden clearly hadn't noticed, however, because Zac found him dozing in front of the TV with Gordon sprawled over his lap. Carefully, Zac resumed his seat, easing into the space beside Aiden, who shifted as the cushion dipped under Zac's weight and only slowly surfaced.

"Crap, I didn't mean to fall asleep," he said, his voice rough.

"It's okay. You look tired." Zac traced the faint circles under Aiden's eyes with one finger and frowned.

"My sleep's been off lately. Guess it's catching up with me." He smothered a yawn as Zac dropped a kiss on his fuzzy head. "I should probably go."

"You don't have to, you know. It's late, and you're welcome to stay here."

Aiden pulled back, blinking sleepily up at Zac. A shadow flickered in his eyes before he spoke. "You don't mind?"

"Your being here is the last thing I'd mind," Zac said, gently throwing Aiden's own words back at him. He leaned in for a kiss, then murmured against Aiden's lips. "Stay."

He sighed when Aiden brought his hands up and slid his fingers over Zac's beard. Aiden's kisses made Zac's heart pound, his blood rush, and his cock harden, and soon Gordon had stalked away, and Zac was lying flat on the couch, Aiden between his legs.

"Is this okay?" Zac forced himself to ask, then groaned when his groin connected with Aiden's.

"Definitely okay," Aiden murmured. "You feel so good."

Zac rocked up against the body over his, soaking in Aiden's heat. He slid his hands up under Aiden's shirt so he could stroke the skin over his ribs and back. Reaching farther, he tucked his fingers under the waistband of Aiden's jeans. Aiden wrenched his mouth away with a low hiss, then buried his face against Zac's throat and nipped and sucked until Zac thought he'd lose his mind.

"Oh, fuck." His skin blazed as they moved together, their

ragged breaths and muttered curses filling the air, and Aiden so, so hard against him.

Aiden pulled back up onto his knees, his fingers at Zac's belt, and in a flash, Zac's trousers were open. He and Aiden watched each other while Aiden wrapped his fingers around Zac's cock, and both moaned as a shudder rocked Zac's frame.

Reaching for Aiden's belt, Zac's head spun with lust and something headier that made his fingers shake. Always perceptive, Aiden pulled away as Zac fumbled, an unspoken question in his eyes.

"I'm all thumbs," Zac said, his voice breathless. "Want to touch you though." He shivered again when Aiden ran his thumb over the head of Zac's cock. "I need–God. That feels really fucking good."

"It does," Aiden agreed. "I missed you, Zac. Missed this. Kissing you, touching you. I missed the way your voice sounds when we're like this."

"I missed you too, so much. I need to feel you." Zac gasped when Aiden leaned down and kissed him again, his mouth hot and ferocious.

They climbed off the couch and moved quickly through the little flat, kissing and pulling at one another's shirts. They were by the foot of the bed when Zac finally managed to unbuckle Aiden's belt, and they lost themselves in giddy laughter. Aiden stopped laughing after Zac got his button fly open though, and he whined when Zac took him in hand.

Aiden's neck and chest were flushed as they sat together on the mattress. Zac worked his way over that heated skin, pressing his lips against the swirls of black ink. The noise Aiden made when Zac flicked his tongue over Aiden's nipple went straight through Zac's body.

Fuck.

Sliding off the mattress, Zac stripped off the last of his clothes, then sank to his knees. He drew Aiden's jeans and boxer briefs down over his hips and urged Aiden to lift up so Zac could drag the clothing the rest of the way off. He kissed the pale skin he uncovered, working his way lower, at last pressing his lips to Aiden's cock and grinning when the body beneath him jolted.

"God, Zac."

Aiden brought his hands to Zac's hair. The fire burning inside Zac leapt higher as he took Aiden in his mouth, his own cock growing impossibly hard as a mix of curses and pleading rolled out of Aiden. Dropping a hand to touch himself, Zac groaned at the shift in pressure, and the vibrations in his throat made Aiden cry out.

Gently, Aiden tugged at Zac's hair, his movements insistent enough that Zac finally allowed the hot flesh in his mouth to fall away. Aiden reached down and swept Zac back up into a scorching kiss. They fell back together onto the mattress, Aiden stroking Zac, so now he was the one writhing and swearing, even as he kissed whatever skin he could reach. Never had Zac known a hunger as strong.

Aiden licked at Zac's lips. "Want you so much."

"Yes." Zac's voice wavered. "Need you inside me. Stuff's in the nightstand."

He closed his eyes when Aiden broke away, working to control his panting breaths as he pulled himself blindly up the bed. He heard the scrape of the nightstand drawer and forced his lids open again when the lube bottle clicked open. His dick throbbed at the sight of Aiden slicking himself up, eyes glazed as he rolled a condom over his cock. Zac moaned.

Aiden was beside him a moment later, eyes ablaze as Zac spread his legs. Aiden teased him open, lubed fingers pushing and stretching so Zac sank even farther into the mattress. Drunk with lust, he dragged Aiden in for more kisses, desperate for as much contact as he could get.

"Fuck me," he rasped out, then begged until Aiden climbed between his legs.

Pinning Zac down, Aiden rutted slowly into him, that delicious weight almost sending Zac over the edge. Zac ran a hand over

Aiden's ass, then reached farther and traced the tender skin behind Aiden's balls with his fingertips.

Aiden clenched his eyes closed. "Oh-h-h, God. You're gonna make me come," he warned, his voice breathless. He opened his eyes again and pretended to pout at Zac's chuckling. "Fuck, don't laugh at me. I'm so wound up I'm about to blow."

"I'm not laughing at you, baby." Zac's heart swelled as Aiden's eyes went wide. "I want to make you feel good."

Aiden's throat worked. "Zac."

"I know." Zac kissed him, deep and sweet, then pushed Aiden back gently. He gave himself room enough to turn over onto his hands and knees and groaned when Aiden's cock brushed against his ass.

Zac hung his head as Aiden lined their bodies up. Aiden slid inside him slowly, and he rubbed circles into Zac's shoulders and back, turning his muscles to mush until all the strength ran out of Zac's arms. Resting his head on his forearms, Zac pushed back, his body burning in the most delicious way. Rocking forward, Aiden curled over Zac, wrapping one arm around Zac's shoulders and the other around his waist.

"*Zac,*" Aiden said, his voice hoarse. He kissed Zac's shoulders as they moved together.

The ache in Zac's body changed, spreading through him in a blistering wave and lighting him up so his hands shook and his toes curled. He turned his face into the pillow and almost sobbed when Aiden reached down and took Zac in his fist.

"Oh, God. More. Fuck, more, Aiden, please, please."

Aiden drove faster and harder into Zac, grunting with each thrust and pumping Zac until he soared.

"Coming," Zac got out, his voice broken as the world tunneled down around him. He flew and crashed all at the same time, and his bones turned liquid as his cum pulsed over Aiden's fist.

He coasted on soft waves of sensation and whined a little when Aiden pulled out. Aiden turned him over and settled back between Zac's legs, and when he slid into Zac again, Zac gasped, his nerves still ringing from an orgasm that had left him almost too sensitive for more fucking. Zac pulled Aiden in anyway, craving that closeness, his moans soft as Aiden's thrusts lengthened and slowed. Each motion sent shockwaves of pleasure throughout Zac's body.

"Fuck. So good, Zac," Aiden said, his voice a mere thread. "Need you so much."

Zac lifted his knees. He wound his legs around Aiden's hips and used his heels to drive Aiden even deeper, arms tight around Aiden's neck. His heart clenched at Aiden's low cry.

"Come in me," Zac whispered. "Want to feel you, Aiden."

Aiden's thrusting rhythm stuttered then, and he shuddered hard before he buried his face in Zac's neck. Zac held him, muttering soothing nonsense as Aiden rode out his high, and when at last he went still, Zac held on a little tighter.

OoOoO

Zac lay awake that night after Aiden had fallen asleep, one arm around Zac's waist. He wondered what Aiden might be dreaming when his breaths changed, or he murmured softly, and from time to time, Zac brushed his lips against Aiden's fuzz and breathed in the smell of soap and skin and man.

At last, Aiden stirred and woke, inhaling slowly through his nose. He tilted his head back and blinked at Zac in the low light of the beside lamp.

"Hey," he whispered. "What are you doing up? You okay?"

"I'm good. Glad you're here." Zac smiled when Aiden's eyes shone.

"You're not just saying that so I make you breakfast tomorrow, are you?"

"No." Zac chuckled. "You brought scones for breakfast, remember? We can eat those with the rest of the fruit, if you want. There's even chicken sausage in the fridge."

"Cool. I'll make some kind of monster breakfast sandwich." Aiden winked at Zac, but quickly looked sheepish. "Just a reminder

I have to be up by five though, so I'll try to be quiet."

"And miss out on monster sandwiches? Screw that," Zac said. "And I don't care what time you wake me." He laid his hand against the side of Aiden's neck. "What are you doing on Christmas Day? Spending time with your parents?"

"Not this year, as it happens," Aiden said. "They're going to Hawaii with friends." He ducked his head and pressed a kiss against Zac's wrist. "Gia and I are planning a dinner/sleepover thing at her place on Christmas Eve for anyone who's around. I'd love it if you'd come."

Zac smiled. "I'm working on Christmas Eve, but I can be at Gianna's for breakfast. I'll even volunteer to make pancakes *if* you'll fry the bacon again."

Aiden grinned. "Of course. This is probably a good time to tell you that I'll be giving you a box of truffles, too. You know—for Christmas and all."

"Oh, God." Zac laughed. "I suppose that's all right. Especially if you help me eat them, Aiden. If you do that, you can give me as many truffles as you like." And slowly, he closed the space left between them with a tender kiss.

Chapter Eleven

Twelve months later

"Hey, you."

"Hey, yourself." Zac hung his keys on the hook by Aiden's front door followed by his coat onto the rack. "I've got four bottles of wine and a loaf of bread, just like you asked."

"Thank you so much. You're a lifesaver."

Zac carried the cloth bag into the kitchen where Aiden stood at the island, busily rolling out sheets of pasta. He wore a long apron over his jeans and t-shirt, and there was a smudge of flour along one cheek, which was flushed from working by the heat of the oven.

"It's my pleasure." Zac smiled. "How often do I get to say that I helped with dinner, hmm?"

"Any time your boyfriend plans a holiday dinner but forgets to buy both bread and the right kind of wine." Aiden met Zac's kiss with a hum. "I'd have asked Em to bring bread from the Kitchen, but then I'd have to listen to his bitching, and I get enough of that at work."

Zac nodded. He was more nervous about this dinner than he wanted to admit because Aiden had invited Emmett and Sean along with Mark and Owen. Not that Zac disliked Aiden's friends—indeed, he enjoyed Emmett, Sean, and the rest of the crew very much. What Aiden's friends liked to eat wasn't always Zac's idea of fun food, however.

He'd grown bolder with his food choices in the year he'd known Aiden, and he beat himself up much less for enjoying a meal. But the Endless Pastabilities crew were fearless when it came to the business of eating and cooking, and some of the dishes Zac had sampled during their dinners at the Test Kitchen had pushed his limits. He wasn't sure he was up for another evening of foams and emulsions or freeze-dried shavings (of any kind) and savory ice creams.

The familiar, utterly delicious smell of roasting chicken that filled the air in the loft set some of Zac's nerves to rest. "What else can I do to help?"

"I'd love it if you'd chop some herbs." Aiden gestured with his chin at a bundle of rosemary sitting on top of a small cutting board. "Then I can show you how to cut tagliatelle, if you think you're up for it."

Zac threw a look at Aiden, who'd started cranking another sheet of dough through what Zac knew was an ancient and much-loved pasta machine "Do I have to use that thing?"

"No. Once the sheets are ready, I cut the noodles with a knife. Makes them more 'homey', in my opinion." Aiden grinned. "Don't be nervous."

"I'm not," Zac reassured him. "I'm just not sure I want my first effort at cutting pasta to end up on a plate in front of people you cook with."

Aiden snorted. "Em and Sean worked two shifts today, Zac—they've been on the go for at least ten hours. All they'll want tonight is to sit and let someone else do the cooking for a change."

Zac straightened his glasses and moved to Aiden's side. "Good point," he said, eyeing the long, pale sheets laid out before them. "Mark and Owen'll be the same, I'm sure, so yeah, show me what to do."

As predicted, all four of their friends were eager to unwind after they arrived. They ranged around the island with Zac, eating little balls of mozzarella bocconcini with marinated vegetables and chatting while Aiden assembled their dinner.

"Do you ever get tired of cooking?" Owen asked. He speared another marinated mushroom with a cocktail stick and fed it to a smiling Mark. "I mean, you say you're on vacation, but here you are making dinner for all of us."

"The answer is no, believe it or not," Aiden said. He smiled down at the pan of chicken parts he'd been shredding. "I find cooking on my off time very relaxing because there's no expectation other than to enjoy whatever I've made."

"I know Zac enjoys whatever you've made." Mark smirked at Zac's arch glare. "Oh, like you don't? Having a chef in your life is probably the greatest gift a man who is useless in the kitchen could hope for."

"Hey, now, Zac's skills are coming along," Aiden said. "He swaps off with me making dinner a couple times a week, and he helped me make the pasta tonight."

"And, I helped decorate for Christmas." Zac waved at the strings of lights and the tree towering in the corner. "I'm not entirely useless in the domestic arena."

Mark blew a low whistle. "Not bad, Zacarías—your mother is going to be impressed when she hears you're finally learning to do more than make salad."

"Oh, she already knows." Zac shared a smile with Aiden. She'd been very impressed when Aiden had told her how much fun Zac was having learning how to cook. "I believe her exact words were that Aiden is a miracle worker."

"Now that sounds vaguely sexual," Emmett said, "and I, for one, do not want to hear about your freaky sex life." He aimed a grimace Sean's way. "Right, babe?"

"Speak for yourself." Sean winked. "Freaky sex talk about the boss only gets better when his man is the one who cut the noodles."

They spent a long time at the table, savoring the fresh pasta and chicken that Aiden had tossed with pine nuts and sultanas and drizzled with a sauce made from olive oil, roasting pan juices, lemon, and herbs.

"Does it taste better 'cause you helped make it?" Aiden asked Zac, a smile playing about his lips.

"You know, I think it does, now that you say that. Thank you again for suggesting I help." He set his hand against the side of Aiden's neck, his heart full.

"You guys are good together," Emmett mused out of nowhere. His blue eyes twinkled as he watched Aiden refill Zac's glass. "You should buy a big house in the woods and get, like, a bunch of foxhounds."

"Okay, no more wine for you, sweetheart." Sean cast an apologetic look at Zac and Aiden while Owen and Mark laughed. "Don't listen to a word he says, guys."

Emmett scoffed. "It's not like I told them to strip naked and run down the street." He waved a hand in his friends' direction. "It's been a year, and they're obviously perfect for each other. You've said so yourself."

"True, but to *you*, Em, and in private. I won't apologize for talking about you behind your backs though," he added with a wink for Zac and Aiden. "You're pretty great together."

"I agree," Mark piped in and raised his glass. "And I won't hesitate to kick your ass if you move out of the city again, Zac, because we all know how much you love it here."

"We both love it here, so I don't think a big house or woods are in the cards." Aiden's voice was light. "Not much room for bunches of dogs in either of our apartments either."

"Plus we work weird hours," Zac said. "Dogs don't much like being alone. Another cat would probably work out though."

Aiden stared hard at Zac. "*Another* cat?"

"Sure—I think Gordon could use some company. In a place like this," he gestured at the loft around them, "with lots of space and light, and all kinds of places to climb, I'm sure he'd be happy. We'll have to safeguard the tree though because Gordon's a big boy. He could pull that shit down in a heartbeat. Yeah, I think a cat or two in this place with us would be perfect," he said and smiled.

"I like the way you think, Zac, but I draw the line at two." The corners of Aiden's lips twitched despite his words of caution. "I refuse to be the crazy cat guys chasing after each other with lint brushes."

"What the fuck?" Emmett narrowed his eyes. "Did they just agree to move in together or have I had too much to drink?" he asked Sean, who, like Mark and Owen, was too busy laughing to answer.

"Both, Em." Aiden grinned, his eyes never leaving Zac's as he wove their fingers together. "So you're okay with moving in here?"

"Sure," Zac replied. "This place has been in your family a while now, and I think you'll agree when I say it should stay there."

"What about your balcony?" Aiden's brow puckered. "I know how much you love it."

"I do, but I love you more." Zac leaned in and gently knocked his shoulder against Aiden's. "Besides, you've got roof access here. Let's build that deck you've been talking about. We could put a tree out there next year!"

Aiden smiled. "I love you, too. And a tree on the roof is a hell of an idea. You know how much I love a project."

"Yes, I do," Zac said, and the fullness in his chest expanded even more as he leaned over and captured Aiden's lips with his own.

Fin

K. Evan Coles

About K. Evan Coles

K. Evan Coles is a mother and tech pirate by day and a writer by night. She is a dreamer who, with a little hard work and a lot of good coffee, coaxes words out of her head and onto paper.

K. lives in the northeast United States, where she complains bitterly about the winters, but truly loves the region and its diverse, tenacious and deceptively compassionate people. You'll usually find K. nerding out over books, movies and television with friends and family. She's especially proud to be raising her son as part of a new generation of unabashed geeks.

K.'s books explore LGBTQ+ romance in contemporary settings.

Contact

Newsletter: http://eepurl.com/dkyS7P

BookBub: https://www.bookbub.com/profile/k-evan-coles

Goodreads:
https://www.goodreads.com/author/show/16711208.K_Evan_Coles

Instagram: https://www.instagram.com/k.evan.coles/

Pinterest: https://www.pinterest.com/kevancoles/

Facebook:

Profile: https://www.facebook.com/kevancolesauthor/

Page: https://www.facebook.com/ColesKEvan

Group: https://www.facebook.com/groups/kswhiskeywordscafe/

Twitter: https://twitter.com/K_Evan_Coles

Blog: https://kevancoles.com/

Also by K. Evan Coles

Pride Publishing (Totally Entwined Group)

~ Tidal Duology w/ Brigham Vaughn (Novels) ~
Wake
Calm

~ The Speakeasy w/ Brigham Vaughn (Novels) ~
With a Twist
Extra Dirty
Behind the Stick
Straight Up (TBD)

~ Boston Seasons (Novels) ~
Third Time's the Charm
Easy For You To Say (TBD)

Wicked Fingers Press (Self-Published)

~Stealing Hearts (Novellas) ~
Thief of Hearts
Healing Hearts

A Hometown Holiday (Short Story)
Moonlight (Short Story)

Off Topic Press (Self-Published)

Inked in Blood w/ Brigham Vaughn (Short Story)

http://www.kevancoles.com

Author's Note

Thank you for reading! Please add a short review on Amazon and let me know what you thought—I would love to hear from you.

If you enjoyed this book, check out Mark and Owen's story, *Thief of Hearts*, the first book in the Stealing Hearts series, available in paperback on Amazon and in ebook format on Amazon and Kindle Unlimited.

https://www.amazon.com/gp/product/B07NGQP7N1/

Some hearts are made to be stolen.

Mark Mannix doesn't believe in love or romance, which is ironic given his birthday falls on Valentine's Day. As he approaches forty, Mark is perfectly content with his life and nursing career in Boston, and—outside of his long-time friend-with-benefits, Alistair—prefers his hookups to be one-night stands.

When Mark's plans for New Year's Eve fall through, he attends his sister's party and meets Owen Todd, a graphic designer of Caribbean descent. Owen is more than a decade younger than Mark and, at first glance the two men appear to have little in common. The chemistry between them is potent, however, and Mark breaks his no-strings pattern, seeing Owen week after week.

A connection forms between the two men, leaving Mark in uncharted territory and drawn to Owen in ways he's never known before. Even so, Mark continues his hookups with Alistair but is startled when Owen withdraws out of a desire to protect himself. His foundations shaken, Mark must decide if he can watch Owen walk away or … if the time has come to follow his heart in a new direction.

CPSIA information can be obtained
at www.ICGtesting.com
Printed in the USA
BVHW042218180420
577902BV00008B/554